MILES TAYLOR and the GOLDEN CAPE

RISE OF THE ROBOT ARMY

ROBERT VENDITTI ILLUSTRATED BY DUSTY HIGGINS

SIMON & SCHUSTER BOOKS FOR YOUNG READERS
NEW YORK LONDON TORONTO SYDNEY NEW DELHI

For everyone who guided me along the way

—R. V.

For Kahlan and Asher

—D. H.

SIMON & SCHUSTER BOOKS FOR YOUNG READERS
An imprint of Simon & Schuster Children's Publishing Division
1230 Avenue of the Americas, New York, New York 10020

Book design by Greg Stadnyk
The text for this book was set in Lomba.
The illustrations for this book were rendered digitally.
Manufactured in the United States of America / 0516 FFG / First Edition
2 4 6 8 10 9 7 5 3 1
Library of Congress Cataloging-in-Publication Data
Names: Venditti, Robert. Higgins, Dusty, illustrator.
Title: Rise of the robot army / Robert Venditti ; illustrated by Dusty Higgins.
Description: First edition. New York : Simon & Schuster Books for Young Readers, 2016. Series: Miles Taylor and the golden cape ; 2 Summary: Reluctant superhero Miles Taylor battles an army of deadly robots, but struggles to dominate eighth grade at Chapman Middle School, where bullies and unrequited love await.
Identifiers: LCCN 2015039685 ISBN 9781481405577 (hardback)
ISBN 9781481405591 (e-book)
Subjects: CYAC: Superheroes—Fiction. Robots—Fiction. Middle schools—Fiction. Schools—Fiction. BISAC: JUVENILE FICTION / Comics & Graphic Novels / Superheroes. JUVENILE FICTION / Action & Adventure / Survival Stories. JUVENILE FICTION / Social Issues / Friendship.
Classification: LCC PZ7.V5565 Ri 2016 DDC [Fic]—dc23
LC record available at http://lccn.loc.gov/2015039685

ALSO BY ROBERT VENDITTI

Miles Taylor and the Golden Cape:
Attack of the Alien Horde

PROLOGUE

ALL LIVING THINGS, FROM ANT TO ELEPHANT, SHARE the same primary goal: survival.

In his long and decorated career as an officer in the Unites States Army, General Mortimer George Breckenridge had become convinced of this undeniable truth. It's the reason alligators have sharp teeth, cheetahs fast legs, and eagles wings that carry them to the sky.

Survival is also the reason nations since the dawn of civilization have built armies, and it's why men and women have always volunteered to join them. The very best of those men and women—exceedingly skilled individuals like General Breckenridge—are picked as leaders because the rest of civilization understands it will require the very best to ensure their survival in the most desperate of moments. George Washington at Valley Forge during the American Revolution.

George Meade at Gettysburg, the battle that turned the tide of the Civil War. And, of course, the legendary George S. Patton, who charged to the rescue and beat back the Germans at the Battle of the Bulge.

General Breckenridge's father, a military man himself, had designated the very general-ish moniker "George" as the middle name of all three of his sons. Mortimer, the eldest, asserted he was named after Patton, whom his father had served under during World War II. Randall, the middle brother, claimed as his namesake George Washington. Chester, the youngest, hadn't the foggiest clue who George Meade was and joined the navy instead. Mortimer, Randall, and Pa Breckenridge never spoke of Chester again.

Anyway, desperate moments.

Every generation has one, that point in history when civilization teeters on the verge of destruction . . . then rejoices when one hero steps forward to snatch survival from the forces of evil that would otherwise cause the death of everything.

General Breckenridge had always believed—knew down in his marrow—that he was destined to be that person. (Not the death-of-everything causer. The other person—the heroic snatcher of survival.) He had waited his entire life for his desperate moment to come. When extraterrestrial creatures had attacked the city of Atlanta last fall—yes, you read that correctly;

aliens had, in fact, attacked one of the largest metropolitan areas in the United States—the General was sure his moment had arrived at last.

Much to the General's chagrin, however, it proved to be another's time to shine.

On the occasion of his sixtieth birthday (the same age Patton was when he died), the General began to worry that he would end up the most unfortunate type of hero—the kind with no desperate moment to triumph over. Oh, how he worried. Desperately, you might say.

Finally, the General realized what he should have known at the start. All those years spent searching for his desperate moment, and it had been right before his eyes the entire time. As he watched the mechanized infantry he'd built load crates filled with state-of-the-art surveillance equipment into an idling military truck, he knew that his lifetime of waiting had been worth every second. He would not fail.

"The hopes and prayers of liberty-loving people everywhere march with you," the General announced. "So calibrate your weapons, infantry. Then calibrate them two times more. We're hunting the biggest game there is."

"Calibrating," the infantry responded in unison.

The General permitted a tight-lipped smile to fall into line beneath his thick, bottle-brush mustache.

Washington, Meade, and even the legendary Patton himself had never faced a moment as desperate as this. He was about to embark on a campaign against nothing less than the greatest threat the United States of America—and the world—had ever known.

He was declaring war on the wearer of the golden cape.

The General was going to destroy Gilded.

CHAPTER 1

AAAANNNG!

Miles Taylor was a superhero, but he still had to wake up for school.

Miles dropped his hand heavily onto his alarm clock. He rubbed the sleep from his eyes, his mind filling with thoughts of what the new school year had in store for him.

If eighth grade was anything like seventh, he wasn't particularly excited. Rising with the sun. A slapdash breakfast of cereal or toast. Trudging downstairs to wait in front of Cedar Lake Apartments for the bus that was too hot in the summer, too cold in the winter, and too smelly year-round. All for the privilege of spending the next nine months at Chapman Middle School, taking tests, getting homework, and dodging run-ins with local football god and scourge of nonathletic kids everywhere, Craig "the Jammer" Logg.

Ugh.

But at least he was a superhero. Hard as it was sometimes for Miles to believe, he really was. Not a dress-up-for-Halloween-and-pretend superhero. A living, breathing, pound-bad-guys-into-the-dirt superhero. He was the Golden Great. The Halcyon Hero. Atlanta's Twenty-Four-Karat Champion. He was Gilded, the only for-real superhero the world had ever seen.

Miles rolled out of bed and headed for the bathroom mirror. He frowned at his reflection. It'd be nice if looking back at him was Gilded, the barrel-chested, six-foot-plus exemplar of good. Instead, all he saw was an average eighth grader from suburban Atlanta who presently had a particularly painful zit asserting itself on his nose.

Miles would've liked to tell the world that he was the hero who, for the past year, had kept Atlanta safe. It was Miles who'd foiled robberies, doused infernos, and even flown apart a tornado. It was he who'd saved the greater Atlanta area—and the rest of humanity—from planetary annihilation at the hands of Lord Commander Calamity and his horde of alien, lizard-monster warriors called the Unnd.

(Seventh grade had been a busy year.)

But Miles couldn't let anyone know those things. Letting anyone know was the ultimate no-no. An old man—the man who'd clandestinely served as Gilded for decades; who'd captivated the minds of every man, woman, and child; who'd been the focus of newspaper articles, TV reports, and comic books beyond number—had told Miles so. He'd warned Miles with his dying breath, imparting that one piece of wisdom before giving Miles the golden cape and changing his life forever.

The golden cape. The source of all of Miles's powers. Miles smiled as he remembered the way he'd felt the first time he'd clasped the cape around his neck. It had transformed him from a nobody into the ultimate somebody. It allowed him to fly, run faster than the eye could see, and lift . . . Actually, he wasn't sure how much weight he could lift. He'd hoisted a full water tower once, but he hadn't been able to find anything heavier to test himself against.

He'd definitely tested his toughness, though. He'd been punched, hit with a baseball bat, and shot by an alien death ray without shedding a single drop of blood. With the cape, Miles could do anything.

Anything good, at least.

Miles brushed his teeth and spat a glob of toothpaste into the sink. The Gilded cape came with a catch. A safety feature. It granted powers to him only if he used it for good.

Simple enough. Like everyone else, Miles wanted to be a hero, didn't he?

Sure, but also like everyone else, Miles wanted to be rich, famous, and have a packed social calendar. Too bad the cape didn't let him use it to acquire any of those things. Miles had learned that through trial and error (mostly error) and with the help of his best friend and confidant, Henry Matte.

Miles walked to his dresser. He took socks from his sock drawer, jeans from his jeans drawer, and a T-shirt from his T-shirt drawer. (Collared shirts were hung in the closet, where they wouldn't get creased from being folded. Like everything else in his life, Miles liked his clothes to be just so.)

Whenever Miles saw his organized clothes, he was reminded of Henry. Probably because Henry had never organized anything in his life. Miles thought of how he'd tried to keep secret that he'd become the new Gilded. He'd almost made it one whole day. But he had figured out very quickly that he needed help. Henry, a super-genius Gilded fanatic whom Miles had crossed paths with in a school bathroom, turned out to be just the kid to give it to him. Together, they'd figured out how the cape worked, and they'd been a team ever since.

It was because Miles understood what the cape

would and wouldn't allow him to do that he combed his mouse-brown hair and pulled on his socks, jeans, and T-shirt at the same speed as every other kid ever. It was also the reason he didn't use the cape to dash to Vermont for a stack of those flapjacks with fresh maple syrup he'd heard about and was instead going to start the new school year with an ordinary breakfast of Cheerios and milk drunk from a glass. Because why bother with having to wash a spoon?

Miles grabbed his backpack and opened his bedroom door.

The glorious sounds and aromas that greeted him indicated this morning was going to be anything but ordinary. He heard the popping of bacon frying in a pan, accompanied by the cheery *whop-whopwhop* of eggs being whisked in a mixing bowl. And he'd eaten enough Southern breakfasts to recognize the scent of biscuits baking in an oven.

These were things Miles hadn't enjoyed since before his mom had traded in him and his dad for a moneyed accountant and moved to South Florida. After that, meals had been handled by Mr. Taylor, the innovative culinary mind who'd invented the concept of cereal served in a drinking glass. Not that Miles blamed him. A master electrician at Atlanta Voltco, Hollis Taylor worked long hours to keep the roof of their cramped, two-bedroom apartment over their heads. That left little opportunity for playing chef. Nevertheless, maybe he'd found time to up his game.

Stomach growling, Miles bounded down the hall toward the kitchen. "Dad? Do I smell country ham?"

When Miles saw who was doing the cooking, he stopped short. It wasn't his dad at the stove. It was the next-door neighbor, Dawn Collins.

"Good nose," Dawn said, beaming. "Big day today, Mr. Eighth Grader. I told your dad I thought you could stand to start your morning right." She tipped a mixing bowl full of beaten eggs into a frying pan coated with a rich sheen of melted butter.

Mr. Taylor looked up from setting the table—Dixie plates and folded paper towels arranged with care. He rubbed a hand through his trimmed beard and shifted his feet. He seemed to get fidgety whenever Miles saw him and Dawn together, an increasingly common occurrence of late.

"I finally took Dawn up on her offer to fix us a meal. Isn't that neighborly of her?" Mr. Taylor locked eyes with Miles and nodded at Dawn, as if to prod Miles into giving a proper show of thanks.

Miles didn't need the prodding. "Absolutely."

Even before Mr. Taylor had become friendly with Dawn, Miles had liked her. She had a generous smile and made the best sweet tea he'd ever tasted.

She was also the only person who'd welcomed Miles and Mr. Taylor when they'd moved into Cedar Lake Apartments the summer before Miles started seventh grade.

Up until a year ago, Dawn had been married to a no-account named Tom Collins. The last time Miles had seen him was the morning he'd overheard Mr. Collins berating Dawn for botching his breakfast. Worried for Dawn's safety, Miles had put on the cape for the first time and burst into apartment 2G as Gilded. He'd explained to Mr. Collins in no uncertain terms that he wasn't to be mean to Dawn ever again. Mr. Collins had lit out that afternoon, Dawn happily went from Mrs. to Ms., and Cedar Lake Apartments was all the better for it.

Watching Dawn drain bacon, stir eggs, and pull biscuits from the oven with ease, Miles couldn't help wondering if her treatment of Mr. Collins's breakfast had been a show of defiance. She definitely knew how to drive a stove.

"You two sit," Dawn said, turning off the burners. She carried the frying pan to the table and spooned eggs onto the plates.

You didn't have to tell a Taylor twice. Miles plopped his backpack on the floor and was reaching for his fork even before his butt hit the chair.

"Everything looks great, Dawn." Mr. Taylor

smiled hungrily, pushing bacon and two biscuits onto his plate. He raised his plastic cup of orange juice. "A toast. To a breakfast that isn't toast."

Miles clunked his cup against his dad's. "I'll drink to that."

"Wait!" Dawn shrieked.

Mr. Taylor jolted and dropped a forkful of eggs onto his lap.

"I forgot the finishing touch." Dawn hurried to the freezer. She reached in and pulled out an ice cube tray. She cracked a pair of cubes shaped like peaches into each of their drinks. Dawn's prized collection of novelty ice cube molds was ever growing, and she seemed to have one for every occasion. If she was keeping her trays in Mr. Taylor's freezer, things were getting serious.

"Peaches?" Mr. Taylor asked, plucking the eggs from his work pants.

"August is National Peach Month," Dawn said with a grin. "We do live in the Peach State, after all."

Every occasion.

Mr. Taylor shrugged. "Good enough for me. Sit down and join us. Miles and me can't polish off this spread by ourselves."

Dawn looked around hesitantly. "Um . . . where should I sit?"

Mr. Taylor had purchased their tiny dinette set for fifteen dollars at a garage sale because the full dining table from the old Taylor homestead was too big for the apartment. The set had come with only two chairs. This was the first time they'd ever needed a third.

"Shoot," Mr. Taylor said, frowning. "Here, take my spot." He started to stand.

Dawn placed a hand on his shoulder, easing him back down. "Nonsense. I need to leave for work anyway."

Dawn had recently earned a coveted waitressing spot during a shift with better tips at the Biscuit Barrel just down the street. Sinking his teeth into a piping-hot, scratch-made biscuit, Miles wondered how long it'd be before the manager wised up and had her switch aprons with the cook.

"You're on your own for cleanup," Dawn said. Then she leaned down and pecked Mr. Taylor on top of his head. With that, she was out the door.

Miles and his dad sat in uncomfortable silence. Mr. Taylor wouldn't look up, but Miles could tell his cheeks were burning red enough to fry eggs over easy. Mr. Taylor was embarrassed, like a kid caught smooching his girlfriend beneath the gym bleachers. Hollis and Dawn, sitting in a tree, K-I-S-S-I-N-G.

It was kind of awkward, Miles seeing his dad dating. Like he was peeking through a window at something he wasn't meant to watch. But it was kind of awesome, too. "It's okay, Dad," Miles said. "She's really nice. She's amazing, actually."

Mr. Taylor sat back in his chair, relieved. "She is, isn't she? Heck if I know what she wants with me." He smiled a bemused smile that Miles understood meant he was kidding but wasn't kidding, too. "Wooing girls has never been my strong suit. Just ask your mother." He leaned over his plate and forked a hunk of country ham.

"Think she can make corn bread?"

Corn bread was a Taylor favorite. Miles's mom had tried to make it once, but she'd baked it dry as a clay brick.

It wasn't that Miles's mom was bad. She was his mom, and he loved her. She and Miles's dad just weren't good together. No one was to blame—things just worked out that way sometimes.

Last Friday, when Miles had had his weekly phone call with his mom, he'd told her about Dawn. It had felt weird to talk about it with her, like he was telling her that her replacement had been hired.

Everyone deserves to be happy, she'd said.

Part of Miles wished her idea of happiness wasn't

married to a CPA seven hundred miles away.

"I think Dawn can do just about anything," Mr. Taylor answered.

Mr. Taylor was entitled to happiness, too, and Miles truly hoped he'd found it. Sitting at their tiny table with a heaping breakfast between them, Miles thought about how far they'd come together. For the first time in a long time, everything seemed right with the world. Miles had a genuinely positive feeling. About himself. About life. About everything. The Taylor boys could take their lumps, but you couldn't keep them down.

"I've been meaning to talk to you," Mr. Taylor said. "About school."

Positive feeling: gone.

"Summer break is over. I gave you a lot of leeway these past three months, but it's time to get back to focusing on your studies. The days of being a superhero all the time are over." Mr. Taylor glanced at the clock on the kitchen wall. "Eight twenty-two a.m., and I've already said something completely ludicrous. That might be a new record."

Right. In addition to Henry, Miles had also revealed to his dad that he was moonlighting as a superhero courtesy of the golden cape that—literally—could do no wrong. Miles remembered the stupefied expression on his dad's face the first time he saw Miles transform. It was the total opposite of the way his dad looked now, talking matter-of-factly about Miles's one-of-a-kind pastime over breakfast. Miles probably wasn't supposed to let his dad know, but he didn't beat himself up about it. Who was to say the old man who'd passed the Gilded mantle on to him hadn't ever told anyone? Sure, he'd instructed Miles not to, but grown-ups were notoriously espousing the do-as-I-say-not-as-I-do philosophy.

Besides, Miles hadn't had much choice. It was either let his dad know on the spot, or be forced to head for the hills with him and Dawn when the Unnd had attacked the city last fall. And anyway, there were more than seven billion people in the world, but Miles had told only a measly two. All things considered, he had a pretty good average. He hadn't even told Josie Campobasso. If that wasn't a heroic show of restraint, what was?

Josie. If there was one person Miles wanted to let in on his secret, it was Josie. She was the most perfect girl to ever set foot—

"Miles? Are you listening?" Mr. Taylor asked.

"Hm?"

"I said, when seventh grade ended, you and I made a deal. I'd lay off and let you have the summer to practice with the cape. Get more comfortable with the heavy workload of looking after the city, so you could be ready when something really bad happens. Tell you the truth, I couldn't be prouder of how you've done. But you're in eighth grade now. Your last year before high school. I want you focusing on your schoolwork first and foremost. Let the police and fire department handle what they can. Your job is to handle what they can't. And *only* what they can't.

"You do that, and when the big things come up, I'll cover for you missing school. Which, unless I'm mistaken, makes me the only dad in America who'll help his thirteen-year-old cut class. Remember that come Father's Day."

"I know it's not easy, Dad. Dealing with me being Gilded. So thanks."

Miles meant it. When it came to fatherhood, this was seriously uncharted territory. It wasn't like Mr. Taylor could go to the library and check out *The Single Parent's Guide to Raising a Superhero.*

Mr. Taylor set down his fork. "I understand you have important boots to fill—Lord, isn't that an understatement—but I want your word it won't get in the way of school any more than it has to." Mr. Taylor held forward his hand. "Let's shake on it."

In the Taylor household, shaking hands sealed an agreement tighter than a presidential signature.

Miles clasped Mr. Taylor's hand. "I promise, Dad." He felt a pang of loss. A few months ago the summer had seemed to stretch out in front of him like an endless highway. Now all that road was in his rearview. How had it gone by so fast?

Mr. Taylor went back to his breakfast. "Good man. After eighth grade comes high school. After that, college. Not a bit of that is negotiable. Because, unless there's something you're not telling me, being Gilded isn't ever going to put food on your table."

Another truth. For all the cape's abilities, making money wasn't one of them. Using it for personal profit was another no-no. All the comic books, toys, and other merchandise based on Gilded were done without consent. Henry had explained the legalese of it to Miles. Something to do with Gilded being a public figure like the president, so his likeness wasn't protected. It sounded fishy, but what was Miles going to do about it, file a lawsuit?

"But what if—"

"I don't want to hear it. My tax bill hasn't gone down, so I'm guessing that means there's still cops and firefighters in this town. Let them do what they get paid to. You think dispatch sends me out every time someone needs to replace a lightbulb?"

"No."

"Darn right, no. I handle the big jobs. Everyone else can pitch in on the rest. That's what I expect of you."

"All right," Miles said glumly. "I will."

"I expect so. Don't forget you gave me your word on this. A man doesn't have his word—"

"—he doesn't have jack." A tried-and-true Hollis Taylor proverb. Right up there with "Better to have it and not need it than to need it and not have it" and "If you don't like Johnny Cash music, I don't want to know you."

Miles pushed his half-eaten breakfast around on his plate. All this talk of not being Gilded had ruined his appetite. He stood from the table. "Speaking of school, I'd better get going. The bus will be here soon."

"You sure?" Mr. Taylor looked surprised. "No telling when we'll eat like this again."

"Yeah. I'm not hungry."

"You go on, then. Have a good day. As for me"—Mr. Taylor reached for Miles's plate—"I vow to not let this good bacon go to waste."

Miles picked up his backpack. The backpack that went everywhere he did. The backpack that held far more than books and notebook paper. He settled it onto his shoulders, feeling the soft hum of its contents against his body.

All his worries vanished. No matter what else happened, he was Gilded. And as long as that was true, nothing could ever go wrong.

CHAPTER 2

AS MILES STEPPED OFF THE BUS, HE THOUGHT about his summer adventures. Was Mr. Taylor honestly all that surprised Miles had spent the months tackling every mess in Atlanta, no matter how small?

The plain, simple truth? Being Gilded was fun.

No, county fairs were fun. Getting pulled in an inner tube behind a pontoon boat on Lake Lanier was fun.

Being Gilded was *spectacular.* Way better than being just another thirteen-year-old filing into his first day of school.

What a difference a year made.

When Miles had arrived at Chapman Middle for his first day of seventh grade, he'd never felt more abandoned and out of place. He was the new kid. He didn't have any friends, and no one was lining up to change that. His life would've continued that way—maybe forever—if not for the cape. Now here he was one year later. Whether the rest of the kids realized it or not, Miles Taylor was their hero.

"Miles! Wait up!"

Miles turned and saw Henry trotting up to him. He was fumbling through his shoulder bag, which was already overstuffed, despite that he hadn't been to his first class of the year yet and shouldn't have had any papers or books to tote around. That was Henry. As neat and organized as Miles was, Henry was the polar opposite. His bedroom looked like a bomb site after a hurricane had blown through. It was a wonder he and Miles were able to function as a team at all.

Still, Miles couldn't help but smile. After they'd spent the summer together, the two of them working to keep Atlanta safe, Miles was happy to see him on school grounds. It reminded him that even though summer was over, the good times didn't have to be.

"Hey, Henry," Miles said. A scrap of paper tumbled out of Henry's bag and floated to the ground. "You dropped something."

Henry continued rooting around in his bag, moving aside the thicket of papers, comic books, charging cords, and other odds and ends. "I know I didn't leave my phone at home. . . ." Then he stopped and grinned, as though he'd told a joke that only he'd heard. "Oh, right." He moved aside his bag to reveal a small pouch hanging on his hip, his smartphone nestled inside.

"Check it out. I bought a phone holster. Instant access whenever I need it. No more digging in my bag. Cool, right?"

Henry Matte, the only human being under the age of sixty who'd ever used "phone holster" and "cool" in the same sentence.

"Good thinking," Miles said, nodding. He conjured an image of Henry being as quick on the draw as a Wild West sheriff, except armed with information instead of bullets. Miles reached into his pocket and pulled out his own smartphone. "Got mine right here."

Miles checked the screen.

No missed calls. No messages.

Miles's phone was his twenty-four-hours-per-day, seven-days-per-week connection to Henry and, by extension, anything and everything the city might need a superhero for (which, in a city as large as Atlanta, turned out to be quite a few things). Using his phone, Henry kept tabs on the various local news outlets and social media sites that were always first to report when and where a crisis was taking place. If something occurred that needed Gilded's attention, Henry sent an alert to Miles, and away Miles went.

There was a time not long ago when Miles had to keep his phone a secret from his dad. But one of the perks of revealing his superhero identity to Mr.

Taylor was that his dad had backed off his stance against his son carrying a phone. Figuring Miles was probably the only middle schooler in creation with a life important enough to actually warrant a dedicated phone line, Mr. Taylor had squeezed the cost of the monthly bill out of the already tight household budget. Now Miles had a smartphone with a data plan, a vast improvement over the bare-bones flip-model phone Henry had surreptitiously financed in the early days when Mr. Taylor was still in the dark.

"What about the . . . you know." Henry glanced around warily, making sure no one was in earshot. There was no such thing as "too careful" when talking about the cape.

Miles reached back and patted the bottom of his backpack. "Packed and ready to go. Just say when."

"We're a well-oiled machine!" Henry crowed.

Henry's excitement level was high, even for him. He lived for school—he always said learning was his favorite pastime. Though he had other things on his mind, Miles agreed this was going to be a year to remember. It didn't have to be just about tests and homework and smelly buses. Not for Miles Taylor. Not for Gilded.

"Let's do this!" Miles said, grinning. He and Henry bumped fists like the teammates they were. "This year belongs to us!"

Miles slid his phone back into his pocket . . . but not before glancing at the screen again.

No missed calls. No messages.

Not entirely unusual. Mornings were always the slowest times for emergencies, particularly crimes in progress. Maybe crooks liked to sleep in, same as everyone else. Besides, Henry was standing right in front of him. If any crises were happening, he'd just tell him.

Miles glided past the kids milling about in the hall. Just by looking, he could tell the difference between the returning students bummed about another year at Chapman and the new students nervous and trying to orient themselves in such uninviting surroundings. Once he'd been the latter. When he'd woken this morning, he'd felt certain he was going to be the former. Being here now, however, he realized he was neither. He was confident and comfortable. A fighter pilot owning the sky with Henry as his wingman.

As if to prove the point, Miles spied Josie Campobasso walking toward him.

Josie. She was the sort of girl you knew had walked into a room not because you saw her, but because you saw the reactions of everyone around you. A straight-A student and a drop-dead knockout, she somehow remained kind enough not to lord her brains or beauty over the less gifted. (Which was everyone.) Josie was perfect. She was unattainable. And right now she was voluntarily approaching Miles to talk to him.

Wonders never ceased.

"Do you come here often?" Miles said with a smirk.

"Very funny." Josie fell in alongside Miles, matching him stride for stride. "Here we go again, right? Bye-bye summer and being able to hang out whenever we want."

Yes, you read that correctly. Much to the annoyance of Josie's friends and the confusion of everyone else (including, if he was being honest, Miles himself), Miles had spent time with Josie over the summer. The most popular girl in school and the boy whom everyone would vote Most Likely Not to Be Voted for Anything had become an item. Miles wouldn't go so far as to label himself her boyfriend, but he was definitely something.

Josie was Henry's down-the-street neighbor in the Estates at Oak Glen, the fanciest subdivision in the county. Since Miles was often at Henry's on Gilded business during the summer, he'd capitalized on the opportunity to get closer to her. The best Miles could understand it, she'd been drawn to him because he was the new kid. He was different. Miles would've preferred to get her attention because he was handsome or charismatic or even bad-boy mysterious, but different was better than nothing. When a girl like Josie is interested in you, it's best not to get too hung up on the whys.

Josie smiled at Miles with her warm hazel eyes. "We have first-period social studies together. Want to see if we can get desks next to each other?"

"Sorry, Josie," Henry answered, his eyes close to his phone. "I have a different homeroom. But maybe Miles has social studies with you."

Miles stifled a laugh. Henry was good at a lot of things, but multitasking wasn't one of them. When he was wrapped up in his phone, he could walk off a bridge and not know it until he hit the water. "Desks next to each other sounds great."

Josie looped her arms through Miles's. "I'll show you the way."

His best friend to his left, the best girl to his right, and the power of a superhero stashed inside his backpack. There was nothing in all creation that could ruin such a perfect moment.

"Hey, Camp-o-bass-o!" a voiced boomed.

Correction: nothing, except the Jammer.

Miles stopped, turned, and looked up into the chest, and then looked up some more into the shoulders, before looking all the way up at the head of the tall, broad person towering over him.

Impossibly—inexplicably—Craig "the Jammer" Logg had managed to increase in size during the summer. Craig was considered by his parents, Coach Lineman, and anyone who knew anything about local football as the most lethal linebacker to ever step cleat on the Chapman Raiders field. Miles just considered him the enemy.

Standing at his side was a smaller member of the Raiders. Miles didn't know the kid's name, and the only word Miles had ever heard him speak was "dude." The kid seemed to orbit around Craig like a moon caught in Craig's gravitational pull.

Craig nudged Josie like the two of them were in a huddle. "Hiya, Camp-o-bass-o," he said with a wink. He always drew out Josie's name when he said it. Probably, he thought it was charming. It wasn't. "You putting in community service hours spending time with these losers?"

"Dude," Dude the Teammate said to Josie, nodding. Dude may have had only one word in his vocabulary, but he was able to apply it to nearly every social interaction. Here he'd made it sound like a polite greeting. If you overlooked the fact that he'd just referred to Josie as "dude."

"Chick," Josie said, nodding right back. She wasn't one to overlook things.

"Chick!" Craig elbowed Dude the Teammate in the ribs and guffawed loudly. "She schooled you!"

Dude the Teammate bowed his head, embarrassed.

"Dude . . ." He sighed. Miles almost felt bad for him. All the time he must spend with Craig on and off the field and not even he was safe from the Jammer's taunting.

Henry chafed. "Speaking of losers, Craig, I saw your brain in the lost and found. You should pick it up, in case you need it."

Craig stiffened, eyeing Henry like unfinished business—a loose fumble that needed to be pounced on. "Watch it, Matte. Or—"

"Or what?" Henry pressed. "You're going to cough on me, so I can catch some of your stupid?" Henry was off-limits to Craig, and Craig knew it. It was on account of Henry being an aide for Assistant Principal Harangue. One word to Mr. Harangue that Craig had laid a hand on Henry, and Mr. Harangue would make sure Craig missed the next practice or—heaven forbid—a whole game. The only thing in the world that terrified the Jammer was the possibility of him losing his right to school-sanctioned violence on the football field.

Craig balled his hands into fists the size of footballs. "You . . . you . . . ," he spluttered.

"Yeah?" Henry answered, arms crossed. If he'd had a stepladder, he would've climbed it and stared right into Craig's face.

"RAAAAGH!" Craig exploded. He planted his paw in Miles's chest and sent him sailing backward.

KRANG!

Miles crashed into the wall of lockers behind him. The sharp sound of his body connecting with metal reverberated in the hallway. Miles dropped to the floor, a pain shooting up his side.

"Dude!" Dude the Teammate laughed, pointing at Miles splayed on the terrazzo.

Miles blinked away stars and saw the Jammer looming over him.

"Be careful who you run with, Taylor. Your friends are liable to get you hurt."

Josie stepped in front of Craig, pushing him away. "Get out of here, Craig."

"Hey now." Craig chuckled, raising his hands in mock surrender. "Don't go siccing the *girls* on me, Taylor. I didn't know you had them fighting your battles for you."

Only 179 school days left until summer.

Craig dropped an arm jovially over Dude the Teammate's shoulders and eased away like a shark in search of his next meal. "Later, losers!"

The kids who'd stopped to gawk at the altercation dispersed. None of them said a thing, but they didn't have to. Miles knew what they were thinking. *The Jammer has picked his target for the year, and it isn't me. Good.*

Henry and Josie rushed to Miles's side. "Man,

Miles," Henry said guiltily. "I'm really sorry. I didn't think Craig would go after you like that."

Josie looked Miles over with concern. "Are you hurt?"

Miles leaped to his feet and tried not to wince, hoping that Josie didn't notice he'd failed. "I'm perfect," he snapped.

Josie reached out a hand. "It's okay. You don't have to be embarrassed. Craig is just bigger than you, is all."

Miles turned away, adjusting his backpack on his shoulders. Fat load of good the contents were to him right now. If only the cape would let him grind the Jammer to mulch. Just once. "Gee," Miles said. "Is Craig bigger than me? Thanks, Josie. I never noticed."

"Okay . . . ," Josie said. "I'm going to class, then. I'll see you there."

Miles couldn't bear to look at her. "You go, too, Henry. I'll see you at lunch."

Miles headed back in the direction of the school's entrance. He needed some air.

CHAPTER 3

OUTSIDE IN THE BUS CORRAL, MILES WATCHED THE kids filing past him and into the building. News spread like germs throughout Chapman Middle. By lunchtime everyone would have heard about the incident with the Jammer. An entire summer spent being the city's hero, and the Jammer had turned Miles into a goat in less time than it takes to do the opening coin toss at a football game. Miles had been an idiot to ever think this year was going to be different.

He took his phone from his pocket and checked the screen.

No missed calls. No messages.

Miles noticed the time. Ten minutes until the first-period bell.

It was just after nine o'clock, and morning rush hour would be at full volume right now. Chances were there was something Miles could help with. Should he check? That was supposed to be Henry's job, but who was to say he hadn't missed something? Nobody is perfect.

Just one quick pass through the apps on his phone. What could it hurt?

Miles opened the first app, a live stream of a local TV station with a traffic correspondent named Steve Voyeur. An Atlanta celebrity, he was known for giving play-by-plays of traffic jams with all the zeal of a home-team announcer calling game seven of the World Series.

"I-285 is a *bramble* this morning, drivers! Tell the boss you'll be late to work because the highway gods have graced us with a five-car collision blocking two westbound lanes. It'll be at least an hour before emergency services can untangle this one. A few bumps and bruises but no thankfully serious injuries."

A fender bender where the worst pain anyone suffers is the cost of having to fix their car. Not a crisis so much as an inconvenience. Just the sort of incident Miles had promised his dad he'd leave to the cops and firefighters.

Miles wanted to help, though. More important, he had the power to help. Was he supposed to ignore that? Of course he wasn't. Heroes didn't ignore people in need.

If he was being honest with himself, there was more to it than that. Miles had been Gilded only last night, but he missed it already: the sensation of being a superhero, the joy on the faces of others when he arrived to lend a hand. The feeling of being . . . better.

Miles strode quickly through the bus corral, moving with purpose toward the Dumpster outside the cafeteria. He glanced once over each shoulder to make sure no one was watching him, then hurried out of sight.

Behind the Dumpster, Miles knelt, shrugged off his backpack, and unzipped the pocket. The cape's dazzling, golden light spilled out, bathing him in its glow. No matter how often or for how long he gazed at the cape—and he'd gazed at it plenty—the look of it never grew tiresome. The cape was the most amazing thing in the world—maybe the entire universe—and it was his.

Time to prove he deserved it.

Miles pulled out the cape and dropped it over his shoulders, holding it by the two halves of its clasp. Soft vibrations traveled through his body, making his hair stand on end. The fabric cascaded to the ground, pooling around his feet. The asphalt was filthy and stained, but that didn't matter. The cape was incapable of getting dirty. It couldn't get wet or torn or burned. It couldn't be anything other than flawless.

God, he loved wearing it.

For a split second the cape flickered like a lamp with a faulty power cord.

Miles focused. He imagined all the people who might be stuck in the traffic jam right now, needing Gilded's help.

A young woman wanting desperately not to be late for the first day at her new job, a job she needed and that took her six months to find.

The cape hummed back to life.

A grandfather excited about taking his young grandchildren to see the whale sharks and penguins at Georgia Aquarium, but now his car was overheating far from home.

The humming grew stronger.

A couple—pregnant wife in labor, husband clutching the steering wheel—as they inched far too slowly toward the exit that would take them to the hospital at last.

The humming reached a crescendo. Miles brought the halves of the clasp closer, feeling them pull at each other. They wanted to touch. They wanted to be whole. They wanted to unleash the incredible power of the golden cape and transform Miles into—

This is Steve Voyeur back with your traffic update.
I-285 doesn't appear to be easing up any time soon, morning commuters.
Guess we'll all be here for the long haul.
WHAT WAS THAT?

LOOKS LIKE YOU NEED THE HELP OF A SUPERHERO!
WHOA!
IT'S GILDED!
?

I'LL GET THESE PEOPLE MOVING AGAIN!

IT'LL ONLY--
--TAKE A--
--SECOND.

READY.

BLESS YOU, GILDED! BUT DON'T WORRY ABOUT ME.
ALLOW THESE FINE MEDICAL PROFESSIONALS TO DO THEIR JOB.
ARE YOU SURE, MA'AM?
DIRECT CONTACT WITH TARGET AT 9:16 A.M. ANALYZING.

9:16?!
I'M CUTTING IT CLOSE!

CAN YOU HANDLE THE REST WITHOUT ME? I KIND OF HAVE SOMEPLACE I NEED TO...

WHY ARE THOSE PEOPLE WATCHING US FROM THE TREES?
OH, UM... THEY'RE JUST A **NEWS CREW**. THE FIREMEN TOLD THEM THEY HAD TO STAY OUT OF THE WAY.
I GUESS THAT MAKES SENSE...

YOU SAID YOU HAD SOMEWHERE TO GO?
RIGHT!

GLAD I COULD HELP!

"TARGET IS HEADING *NORTHEAST.*"

Miles was crouched with the cape in his hands. He really hoped changing behind Dumpsters wasn't becoming a thing.

On second thought, he didn't care. It was worth it to wear the cape and get away from Chapman and the Jammer and every other thing that was crummy about being a kid instead of a superhero.

What about the people he'd spotted in the trees, though? That was weird. The press usually ran straight at him, waving their arms and shouting for him to pose for a photo, or give them an interview, or autograph their forehead. (No joke. A blogger had asked him to do that once.) Since when did they hide?

Rrriiinnng!

The first-period bell! Miles was late. If Mr. Essaye gave him after-school detention, his dad would be sure to figure out why.

Miles stuffed the cape inside his backpack and sprinted for the building.

CHAPTER 4

"YOU'RE LATE."

Turned out, it wasn't Mr. Essaye who Miles should have been worried about. It was Henry.

Don't let appearances fool you. Henry Matte was barely five feet tall, and his bulky glasses were way too large for his head. But when it came to disapproving glares like the one he was giving Miles now, he was a giant among eighth graders.

"How do you miss the bell on your first day?"

Miles was bent over in the hallway, hands on his knees as he caught his breath. Putting in daily workouts as a superhero didn't do much to bolster his own physical conditioning. Inhaling the fumes from Chapman Middle's harsh floor disinfectant didn't help much, either.

"Henry." He wheezed. "Glad you're here. I don't have any hall passes. Can you doctor one up to get me into first period?"

Henry raised an eyebrow. "We need to be careful how often you use those. I go into Mr. Harangue's desk for them too often, he's going to notice."

Henry was head of new student orientation, which offered him even more access to Mr. Harangue's office. It also allowed him to roam the halls, whether he was on official business or not. Teachers took it on faith that he had permission to be wherever he was. Why wouldn't they? He looked about as nefarious as a chipmunk. A baby chipmunk. With thick-framed glasses.

"I know," Miles said sheepishly. "But I'm in a tight spot. Help me out."

Henry narrowed his eyes and scanned the hallway. "Not here."

Miles followed Henry into a nearby bathroom. It was a wise choice of venue for a clandestine meeting. No one ever entered a middle-school bathroom unless they absolutely had to.

Henry checked the stalls to make sure they were alone. Then he reached into his shoulder bag. "Here," he said, passing Miles a handful of hall passes. "But you have to make these last a while. You really need to concentrate on being at school."

Miles slipped the hall passes into his back pocket. "You sound like my dad."

"We can't afford to waste a hall pass because

you're sulking about a run-in with Craig. They're for Gilded missions only."

Miles was offended. He and Henry had been a team for almost a year, and he still acted as though Miles couldn't be responsible. "I *was* on a Gilded mission," he groused.

Henry snatched his smartphone from its holster and cycled through the phone's news apps. "I didn't hear about any priority-one incidents this morning."

On Henry's self-devised threat-level scale, priority one was reserved only for the stuff that required immediate super-heroing. Shoot-outs, runaway trains, and alien invasions all warranted priority one. The scale went all the way to priority five, which was for things like relocating stray, trash-can-raiding bears to the Appalachian Mountains (yes, Miles had actually done that once). Henry had created the system for when there was more than one incident to deal with at the same time, which happened a lot when you were the only superhero in town.

Henry studied the last of the apps. "Nothing. So what mission did you . . . ?" Henry's voice trailed off. Then he scowled at his phone. "No you did not!" He turned the phone around, showing the screen to Miles. "Care to explain this?"

The screen showed the feed from the Gilded Group, a news aggregator for all things Gilded. In the Gilded Group, users shared stories, listed sightings, and otherwise kept tabs on the hero. It was the single most useful tool in Henry's information arsenal. Currently, the lead story was about Gilded clearing a car wreck during the morning rush hour.

Busted.

Miles shrugged. "I figured I'd help."

Henry frowned. "Miles, we've been over this a zillion times. Information processing and dispatch is my responsibility." Henry came up with titles for everything. "Information processing and dispatch" was his way of making "surfing the Internet" and "checking social media sites" sound technical.

"I heard about the accident and decided to fix it," Miles said. "What's the big deal?"

"The *big deal* is that because you intervened, you're late to your *first* class on your *first* day of school. That draws attention to you, and attention is bad. Plus, if I hadn't been waiting to bail you out, you might've wound up in detention. Imagine if a priority-one incident happened while you were stuck in there. Short of puking on Coach Lineman's stopwatch, there'd be absolutely zero chance of you getting excused. Might be a little awkward if you had to turn into a superhero right in front of him, don't you think?"

Miles wondered how many push-ups an in-detention superhero transformation would earn him. Coach Lineman assessed everything in terms of push-ups. It was the only currency he dealt in.

"I'd say you risked an awful lot for very little results," Henry finished.

"The people caught in that traffic jam sure seemed happy with the results. Like this couple rushing to get to the hospital to deliver their first baby, and . . ." Miles trailed off. No, he'd dreamed that up as an excuse to go to the wreck. But it certainly could've been true, right?

Henry raised an eyebrow. "And . . . ?"

"Nothing. I'm just saying people were glad to see me."

"I'm sure they were. Your arrival was *super*-convenient for them." Henry smirked, a sign that his play on words had been intentional and he was proud of it. "But Gilded shouldn't be a convenience. He has to be a necessity."

Then Henry grew serious—wordplay time was over. "Look, Miles. You may be a superhero, but you have to live by the rules. Over the summer you could deal with every little thing that came up. But now that we're in school, we have to be more careful." Henry placed a reassuring hand on Miles's shoulder. "I'm just looking out for you. We're a team, remember?"

"I remember," Miles said. And he did. Yet as much as he and Henry were a team, only one of them understood what it meant to wear the cape.

Henry nodded. "Good. From here on out, keep in mind the reason we set you up with a phone is so it'd be easy for me to reach you. We didn't do it so you could look for reasons to go off on your own."

"Got it."

"If you're going to have a smartphone, be smart about it."

"I said I got it!" Henry sure did know how to belabor a point.

"All right, all right." Henry slid his phone back into its holster. "No emergencies right now, so we can both go to class. See you at lunch."

"Right. Thanks for the passes." Miles turned and walked off.

"Wait!" Henry called out.

Miles turned back to see Henry trotting toward him.

"Almost forgot." Henry reached into his shoulder bag. "I got you a present."

"A present?" Miles's interest was piqued.

"Yep. A *good* one." Henry searched through the bag's contents, frowning. "I know it's in here somewhere. . . ." A gum wrapper and a torn-off movie theater stub fell to the floor. "Got it!" he exclaimed triumphantly. He pulled out a comic book and smoothed it against his chest.

Then he handed it to Miles. "Sorry. It's a little bent."

It was a copy of *Gilded Age*, the monthly series that chronicled Gilded's many fantastic feats. The series had been in print since the late 1950s, when Gilded had first appeared on the scene. Original copies of the early issues were difficult to come by and just as difficult to afford. Not even Henry had them all, much to his undying chagrin.

The comic book Henry handed to Miles wasn't worth much at all, though. On account of the creases and other damage—was that a smear of caramel sauce or rubber cement on the cover?—it wasn't even worth the newsstand cover price. But to Miles it was more precious than every other issue of *Gilded Age* combined. Because the story in *Gilded Age* number 687 was about him.

"Your first time in print," Henry said, grinning. "Congratulations."

Miles gazed at the cover, an artist's rendition of Gilded—Miles—battling Lord Commander Calamity. The artist must've used photo reference because the Lord Commander looked strikingly, frighteningly real. He was targeting Miles—Gilded—with his weapon, a cross between a battle-ax and a spear that had the added pleasure of firing death-ray blasts (because apparently regular battle-axes and spears weren't deadly enough for the Lord Commander). Miles massaged his chest, remembering the searing, red-hot agony he'd felt when one of the blasts had burned into him. Not even the cape had been able to insulate him from that pain.

The cover copy read ATTACK OF THE ALIEN HORDE! A SPECIAL DOUBLE-SIZED COMMEMORATIVE ISSUE!

Miles was dumbstruck. Holding the comic was nothing short of surreal. "When . . . ?"

"It should be in stores later this week," Henry said. "I'm a subscriber, so my copy was mailed to me early. Honestly, I expected them to release the story a long time ago. I mean, it's been almost a year since it happened, right? Turns out the government tried banning the publisher from printing it because they said it contained classified information. The publisher filed a lawsuit in defense of their First Amendment right to freedom of the press. And now there you are."

Henry had just invoked the phrases "classified information," "First Amendment," and "freedom of the press" in relation to Miles. This was weirder than the first time he'd seen himself as Gilded on the evening news. Then again, that hadn't involved the freaking *Constitution of the United States.*

"Of course, leave it to the press to get the details wrong," Henry continued, frowning. "Some of your dialogue is off. And look"—he took the comic book back from Miles and flipped through the pages—"they didn't even bother to show me and your dad helping you."

The Lord Commander had felled Miles with a pair of energy blasts and was about to deal the deathblow. Then, out of nowhere, his dad had sped into the fray in his work truck, with Henry riding shotgun. If they hadn't smacked into the Lord Commander and bought Miles some time, Miles might not have recovered. The battle—and maybe the planet—would've been lost.

"That's right . . . ," Miles said. "I forgot about that."

Henry shrugged it off. "You were probably dazed from the fight. But what's the writer's excuse for leaving us out? Would it have killed him to do a little research? I mean, your dad did interviews about it for a month."

Miles remembered that now: the phone in the Taylor household ringing nonstop, reporters from all over the country wanting to talk to his dad.

"Anyway"—Henry handed the comic book back to Miles—"give it a read. All the time we spend poring through back issues of *Gilded Age* to learn what your powers are, now you get to read one about yourself. Imagine, someday the next person to don the golden cape will study *Gilded Age* number six eighty-seven to see what they can learn. And they'll be learning from you. You're part of a grand and noble legacy, Miles. A hero's legacy."

The next person to don the golden cape. Miles had never considered that before. But it made sense. The old man had given the Gilded cape to him, and while Miles was only thirteen right now, someday he'd be old, too. Too old to wear the cape. He'd have to find someone to carry on the responsibility. What would become of Miles then? An emptiness crept over him.

"You all right?" Henry leaned in close, examining Miles. "You're putting a death grip on that comic book."

Miles had nearly crumpled the copy of *Gilded Age* into a wad. He shoved thoughts of legacies and replacements out of his mind. "I'm okay. I should get to class, though. Don't want Mr. Essaye asking too many questions about why I missed roll call. First day of school and all."

Henry slapped Miles on the shoulder in agreement. "Good thinking. See you at lunch?"

"At lunch. And thanks for the present, Henry. For real."

"No problem. Just don't let it go to your head," Henry said with a wink.

CHAPTER 5

THE BIG BREAKTHROUGH HAD OCCURRED WHEN they discovered the spacecraft buried under the onion patch.

The unique soil in Vidalia, Georgia, didn't just make it home to the world-famous Vidalia sweet onion that took its name from the largest city in Toombs County. It also concealed Earth's first confirmed contact with extraterrestrial life, an event that long predated the attack on Atlanta the previous fall. There were only a select few who knew about the latter factoid, though, General Mortimer George Breckenridge chief among them.

The discovery had not come easily. First, the General had needed to answer what was, in his mind, the greatest lingering mystery of the alien attack on Atlanta: Who was the old man found dead in the parking garage?

General Breckenridge could have assumed what the emergency services personnel on the scene did—that the man was just an average Joe who had sadly been in the wrong place at the moment Gilded and the alien had crashed into the garage, bringing a mountain of rubble down on his poor, average-Joe head. It had been a titanic struggle, Gilded wrestling midair with the monstrous beast that even a second lieutenant fresh out of Officer Candidate School would have recognized as a solo scout on a mission of reconnaissance for a larger invading force.

After the invasion, all attention had been paid to the aliens themselves. But something about Average Joe nagged at the General. How had he happened to be in the garage at that moment? Why had he not been carrying any identification? Why had no one seen him before?

Even though the General had lately resorted to using operatives from the Central Intelligence Agency to help him build a dossier on Gilded, he had little affinity for spy games. Why lurk in the shadows when you can ride in style in an M1 Abrams tank? Nevertheless, he knew secrecy when he smelled it. And Average Joe reeked of secrecy.

General Breckenridge assigned a team to ferret out Average Joe's identity. They started by hacking into the accounts of every power company and telephone provider in the greater Atlanta area, looking for accounts that had gone past due since Average Joe's death.

Illegal? Sure. Accessing that information without permission or a warrant signed by a judge violated more laws than the General cared to count. (Seriously, he didn't care enough to count. He never concerned himself with legality when he deemed national security to be at stake.) But Average Joe's body had been found with no sign of a wedding ring, so there was a chance that wherever he lived, there was no one left to pay the bills.

After cross-referencing the past-due accounts against records from the Department of Motor Vehicles, the team discovered a driver's license photo that matched the old man found in the garage.

Just like that, Average Joe had a name: Donald Plower, born November 19, 1935. His income tax records indicated he was a retired onion farmer from Vidalia, Georgia, who still owned land there. But if he had retired and moved to the city, why did he still have the farm?

Why indeed?

General Breckenridge dispatched a spy drone from Dobbins Air Reserve Base north of Atlanta. It detected an unidentifiable object buried beneath the old Plower farm. That was all the excuse the General needed to enter the United States Army into the onion-growing business.

With Donald Plower now confirmed as deceased, the General called in a few favors. If there's one thing a forty-year career in the military will do, it's introduce you to a lot of people. And if that career leads to you becoming a four-star general, most of those people will be terrified to say "no" when you tell them to do something.

One such terrified person was the second assistant to the deputy mayor of Vidalia, who made sure that the Plower farm went up for auction right away.

The General purchased a straw hat and a pair of overalls, strode in on the day of the auction, and bid three times the fair market value before the auctioneer could utter a single hurried word. The rest of the potential bidders stomped off in a huff, the General signed the deed on behalf of Uncle Sam, and the General had what he wanted without ever considering that the unidentifiable object buried beneath the Plower farm might be a rusted-out Model A Ford.

General Breckenridge was standing in front of that unidentifiable object right now. It was no longer unidentifiable. And it wasn't a Model A Ford.

What the General had dug up (not actually dug up himself, of course, but commanded assorted privates and a corporal to dig up for him) on the Plower farm was so earth-shattering, he'd transported it back to Dobbins in a gutted mobile home to prevent the snooping locals from ever getting a glimpse of it. It was an honest-to-goodness, real-deal ship from outer space. The hull was broken from what must've been a catastrophic impact with the ground, and most of the interior had decayed and leached into the earth long ago. But it was a spacecraft all the same. A craft designed for long, sustained journeying—of the interstellar variety.

It was unquestionably the most significant archaeological find in the history of the human race, but General Breckenridge knew he would never receive credit or recognition for unearthing it. No article in *Archaeology* magazine. No one-hour exposé on the History Channel series *Ancient Aliens*.

No matter. The General didn't care about those things. He didn't want to be known as an archaeologist or an expert on alien culture. He wanted to be known for triumphing in the face of adversity. For rescuing the world during the most desperate of moments. What the spacecraft signaled to him was that his desperate moment had not, as he had feared, passed him by. He had discovered the key to unraveling the secrets of Gilded, a being whose mere existence was a threat to America and the balance of power around the world.

"Nothing but a fraud," General Breckenridge muttered.

"Did you say something, General?" Dr. Marisol Petri asked. Dr. Petri was one of the world's foremost experts in theoretical zoology. The General had originally enlisted her to unlock the mysteries of the strange, reptile-like beings who'd attacked Atlanta. Now he'd sent for her to join him in the hangar, so she could have the privilege of hearing the next phase in his plan while standing in the presence of his greatest accomplishment. So far.

"Gilded," the General said curtly. "He flitted around town in his shiny costume, pretending he was some sort of a hero. But he was no hero. He was an ex-onion farmer who won the equivalent of the galactic lottery. He never even served in the army," the General added. "Does that sound like a hero to you?"

"It seems like all he wants to do is help," Dr. Petri offered.

The General harrumphed through his thick mustache. "That's exactly what he wanted us to believe. All these years, people assumed he was some fantastic being who arrived to deliver us from the ills of the world. If he was so noble and good, why go to such great lengths to conceal his identity?"

"Perhaps he's afraid of what people will do if they know who he really is."

"A coward's excuse. If he ever possessed any integrity at all, he would've come forward the day the spacecraft crashed on his farm. Told us what he knew. Helped us learn if there are more ships like it out there in the universe. Imagine how much better we would've prepared our defenses against alien intervention, if only we knew an interstellar vessel had already crashed within our borders. Instead, he chose a double life. Hid the truth from the good, God-fearing citizens of the United States. There wasn't an honest bone in his body."

Dr. Petri furrowed her brow. "I don't understand, General. Why are you speaking about Gilded in the past tense? Didn't he make an appearance just this morning?"

The General grinned. It was a practiced, informed grin. A grin that came with knowing the classified doings of the most powerful nation on the planet because he was the one who'd set the doings in motion. "That's the first intelligent question you've asked, Doctor."

General Breckenridge reached for a handheld radio hanging on the wall and pressed the talk button. "Corporal, has the data been compiled?"

"Yes, General!" the radio squawked in reply.

"Bring it to me at once." The General returned the radio to its place. "Now, Doctor, you'll see there's no such thing as luck. Luck is what happens when preparation meets opportunity."

"I didn't realize you read the classics, General. That line about luck is my favorite quote from the Roman philosopher Seneca the Younger. It's an abridgement, though. The actual quote is—"

The General waved his hand dismissively. "Eisenhower made the maxim matter."

"You didn't let me finish."

The heat of anger gathered under the starched, spotless collar of the General's shirt. "Are you a five-star general, little lady?"

Sometimes an older Southern gentleman can refer to a younger woman—even a doctor—as "little lady," and instead of being condescending, it will come across as charming in a Southern-gentleman sort of way. The General hoped his tone made it clear this wasn't one of those times.

"No," Dr. Petri said flatly.

"Do you see any five-star generals anywhere in this hangar?"

"No." Dr. Petri didn't bother to glance around before answering. She was trending toward insubordination. The General did not appreciate it one bit.

"Well, then," the General continued, glaring. "As the highest-ranking officer present, my opinion is the one that matters. So you can take it as gospel truth when I say that the most important person who ever uttered those words wasn't Seneca the Younger. It was the stalwart United States Army General Dwight D. Eisenhower, hero of World War Two, who commanded more than one hundred fifty thousand Allied troops in the desperate moment the world has come to refer to as D-day. You don't have anything against Ike, do you?" The General leveled a steely gaze at Dr. Petri. It was a gaze that said, *Choose your next words very carefully.* "I like Ike. Everybody likes Ike."

"Not at all. I believe my grandparents even voted for him. Twice."

"You come from a line of fine Americans." The General let the remainder of his thought go unspoken. *What happened to you?*

The conversation was interrupted by the thudding of boots hurrying across the hangar's bare, concrete floor. General Breckenridge turned to see his aide, a pudgy corporal with pale skin and red cheeks that always looked as though they'd been slapped. The corporal huffed toward him, a rolled-up map stuffed under one arm.

"Corporal," the General stated. The General couldn't recall the corporal's name, but that was what ranks were for. "So glad you could finally join us."

"Yes, General!" Corporal Slapped-Cheeks said cheerily. "I have the map, General!"

The General found it annoying that the corporal had failed to pick up on the tone of the General's voice, a tone that should have made it clear the corporal's arrival wasn't something to be glad about at all, but merely a necessary means to an end. Such imperceptiveness would no doubt ensure he remained a corporal for a very long time. "Would you care to show me the map?" the General asked coldly.

"Yes, General!" Corporal Slapped-Cheeks hurriedly unrolled the map on a table. It showed a grid of the greater Atlanta area. Red dots had been drawn on the paper in numerous places, making the map look as though it had acne.

The corporal pointed a chubby finger at one of the dots. "These indicate each sighting of the target during the last month, either due to incidents generated by us, or the target's standard efforts to patrol the city."

"The target?" Dr. Petri asked hesitantly. "You're talking about Gilded."

The General waved dismissively again, as though he were shooing a bothersome insect.

The corporal unrolled a sheet of clear acetate

crisscrossed with red lines. He laid it over the map, so that one end of each line matched up to one of the red dots. The other ends of the lines all converged in a single area northeast of the city.

"Combining the findings of our own surveillance with reliable information from news reports and civilian accounts, we plotted the flight path the target took when arriving at each incident. As you can see, they almost all lead back to this approximate location." The corporal tapped a large red circle drawn around the area. "Our conclusion is the target is based somewhere in the vicinity of Interstate 85 and Jimmy Carter Boulevard."

The General clasped his hands behind his back. "Jimmy Carter," he said, fuming. "I might've known."

Dr. Petri stepped forward, examining the map and its tangle of dots and lines. "I'm confused."

"Of course you are, little lady." The General didn't try to sound like a Southern gentleman this time, either. "You asked earlier why I was referring to Gilded in the past tense. It's because I was speaking of the Donald Plower version of Gilded. I've concluded that on the day the first alien scout arrived, Mr. Plower transferred possession of the technology that allowed him to become Gilded to a new agent. This new agent is who has been appearing over the course of the last year. And now we know," the

General said, pointing at the red circle on the map, "that the agent is headquartered there."

"Agent?" Dr. Petri looked perplexed. "You think Gilded is a spy?"

"You don't?" The General scoffed again. "A clandestine transfer in a parking garage, with an extraterrestrial attack as cover. If that isn't top-notch spy craft, I don't know what is. Not even the Soviets in their heyday could orchestrate something like that. The issue isn't whether he's a spy, but *who* he's spying *for*. All this 'good' he does, it's to throw us off his scent. He's smart. There's no denying that."

The General turned to Corporal Slapped-Cheeks, who'd been standing silently like a well-trained dog waiting for his master to pay attention to him. "There's an abundance of commercial and residential property in the area, Corporal. The target could be dug in anywhere. We can't move on him until we have a clear window of opportunity. Any missteps, Gilded will relocate, and we'll have to restart the tracking process from square one. Put surveillance cameras on the tallest buildings. I want squads of my mechanized infantry on standby, ready to move in at a moment's notice. Is that clear?"

"Unambiguously, General."

"Then move out."

"Yes, sir!" Corporal Slapped-Cheeks saluted, his

posture straight like a concrete telephone pole—a concrete telephone pole with a jiggly belly. Then he gathered up his maps and scampered off.

General Breckenridge turned to Dr. Petri. "You're dismissed," he declared, as though Dr. Petri were one of his subordinates. Because in every way, he knew she was.

"Pardon?"

"You may return to your lab. The Unites States Army has continued need of your service."

Dr. Petri cleared her throat. "If it's all the same to you, General, it's time I went back home to San Diego. I cataloged and analyzed all of the alien specimens you recovered. I won't be of any more use to you. I'd like to return to my own independent research."

"I'm afraid I can't allow that," the General answered unapologetically. He never apologized for the needs of the country. "There's still the matter of Subject One to deal with."

Dr. Petri shook her head. "Subject One is stable. I told you there hasn't been any change in her condition since she was brought here."

The General's expression soured. "Perhaps. But you still haven't determined the cause of her . . . peculiar ability. And while I don't yet know the identity of the person currently acting as Gilded, I soon will. That much I guarantee. When I do, your expertise may just prove helpful."

"But, General—"

"That will be all, Doctor. My mechanized infantry are waiting outside to escort you back downstairs. And to make sure you stay there."

CHAPTER 6

SLAP!

It was early the next morning, and Miles was looking at a folded-over copy of the *Atlanta Journal-Constitution* that had landed on the dinette table in front of him, interrupting his breakfast of Cheerios in a glass. The headline read, GILDED CLEARS AUTO WRECK.

Mr. Taylor pointed at the paper, his jaw tight. "Tell me I'm not seeing that."

Miles swallowed his mouthful of soggy cereal. "Dad, I—"

"You deliberately went against your word to me. What I want to know from you is why?"

This was no way to start a morning. Miles was already let down by Dawn's absence and the subsequent lack of yesterday's stellar breakfast spread. Now he was fixing to get lectured by his dad for something Henry had already lectured him about. "Do we have to talk about it, Dad? Henry went over it with me yesterday."

"Did he, now? Guess that absolves me of my parental duties, then." Mr. Taylor's tone indicated that was absolutely not the case. "But to answer your question, no, *we* don't have to talk about it. I'm going to talk. You're going to listen."

Miles lifted his glass to gulp down another mouthful of cereal. "Okay."

Mr. Taylor snatched the glass from Miles's hand, nearly sloshing milk and toasted oats down the front of his shirt. "I said, you're going to *listen*."

Miles gulped again, and this time it had nothing to do with cereal. He was in trouble. "I'm sorry I used the cape to clear a traffic jam. I won't do it again."

Mr. Taylor frowned as though Miles was a used-car salesman trying to sell him a lemon for the second time. "Nothing doing. You sat in that same chair yesterday and made me the same promise. We even shook on it, for all the good it did. It wasn't until I saw the paper this morning that I realized you never had any intention of keeping your word."

That wasn't true. Miles really had meant to obey his dad. Hadn't he?

"So," Mr. Taylor continued, "since your promises don't mean anything, I've got no choice but to guarantee you make good. That means for the next two weeks, when you aren't at school, you're with me."

Miles shot out of his chair. "You can't!"

"I can and I will. I'll pick you up out front when school lets out, and you'll come finish my work shift with me. Plenty of time to do your homework. I'll let you keep the cape with you for emergencies, and if something important jumps off, I'll let you take care of it. But otherwise, you won't be leaving my sight."

Miles already had Henry over-managing his use of the cape. Now he'd have to get approval from his dad, too. What next, a babysitter? Miles had proved himself as the city's champion, so why did he still have to take orders from everyone else?

"Dad . . . I spent the summer using the cape as much as I wanted, taking care of everything in the city. Then suddenly it's the first day of school, and that's supposed to change? I got mixed up a little, that's all. Can't you give me a little time to adjust?"

Mr. Taylor sighed. "If I thought that was it, I'd give you the space. I would. But not even an hour went by between our conversation and you heading out like we'd never even talked. That's not a mix-up. It's disobedience. You knew what you were supposed to do. You just decided not to do it. Probably because you thought you'd get away with it. And you would've, too, if I hadn't seen the paper on Dawn's sofa."

Miles's couldn't help but take note. His dad had been to Dawn's apartment, and they'd ventured at least as far as the sofa. The plot thickened.

"Put yourself in my shoes," Mr. Taylor persisted. "Do you know of any other parents contemplating a newspaper subscription so they can make sure their kid is doing what he's supposed to? I sure can't."

Mr. Taylor was dug in like a stubborn tick. Miles was getting the very bad feeling that he wasn't going to change his mind. He had to come up with something. "I've got the phone," he offered. "I'll call you before I go anywhere and again as soon as I get back."

"I wish I could accept that, son. But you're going to have to earn it. You can start by having your butt out front of school as soon as the bell rings for the next two weeks. Convince me you've learned to be a man of your word. And before you say anything else, realize that if it were up to me, I'd make you spend the whole day under my supervision. That's how little I trust you right now. So be glad the school has rules about too many absences."

Miles flopped back down in his chair. He was defeated, and he knew it. He might be bulletproof and bombproof and every-other-thing-proof, but he was no match for a dad with discipline on his mind.

Mr. Taylor lifted his tool belt from the chair by the door. "I'll take your silence as a sign that you understand my instructions. Hurry up and finish your breakfast. I'll be waiting in the truck to drive you to school. I want to see that you actually enter the building." Mr. Taylor left, pulling the door closed after him.

Miles dumped his cereal down the sink.

What was he going to do?

Miles went to his room to get his backpack and saw the copy of *Gilded Age* Henry had given him sitting on his bedside table. He'd meant to show it to his dad, but he'd forgotten. Now, unless his dad said otherwise, the comic book was going to be Miles's only link to Gilded.

Same as every other kid in the world.

CHAPTER 7

A CITY UNDER SIEGE. BUILDINGS AFLAME. Defenseless citizens scream and flee in terror.

Beastly, scaly creatures from beyond the deep black of space. Sharp fangs jut from their snarled maws. Clawed hands wield weapons of murder.

The hero arrives, a blur of gold against the smoke-stained sky. The citizens cry out desperately. *Please, save us!*

But can he? The hero stands alone against a thousand enemies or more. Staggering odds from which no sane being—super or not—would dare to hope for survival. This is humanity's darkest hour.

The battle is joined. Two entities of immeasurable power trading blows with the fate of Earth hinging on the outcome. The ground shudders from the ferocity of their struggle:

Krak!

Whak!

SLAMMM!

Will the villain prevail and burn Earth to a cinder? Or will the hero claim victory and allow the sun to once more shine through the haze of war?

The dust settles, and the world waits with white-knuckled tension to see who reigns supreme.

Could it be?

It is possible?

Yes! There, atop the stricken body of his adversary, the hero stands triumphant. The citizens cheer and weep tears of adoration. *Look!* they exclaim. *A real, genuine SUPERhero!*

He's the embodiment of bravery. An icon of virtue. No other hero before or after will ever compare to—

"Miles? Are you listening?"

Miles looked up from his copy of *Gilded Age* number 687 and saw Josie frowning at him. They were sharing a table during fifth-period study hall in the Chapman Middle library.

"Did you hear anything I just said?" she whispered. Mrs. Binding, the head librarian, was on duty. Mrs. Binding was fair, but tough. There were two things she despised in her library: noise and things not being put back in their place. She and Miles got along just fine.

Miles's cheeks flushed red. "Oh. Sorry." He pointed to the comic book open on the table in front of him. "I was lost in the story."

It was true. It'd been three days since Henry had given him the comic book, and it continued to captivate him no matter how many times he read it, which was a lot. Reading it had helped him pass the time since his last mission clearing up the traffic jam. The city had been experiencing an uncommon bout of peace and relative tranquillity for the past seventy-two hours, and Mr. Taylor was adhering strictly to the terms of Miles's punishment—no big crises, no Gilded.

Until something bad happened and Miles suited up again, he'd just have to settle for reliving his past, which was almost as good as the real thing. Actually, it wasn't anywhere near as good. But it was better than nothing at all.

Josie exhaled shortly, blowing a stray lock of her chestnut hair to the side. "I was telling you that the park is having a bird-watching hike today at six o'clock. If your dad can drop you off, my mom said she'd take you home after. We can share my binoculars."

Josie was an avid birder. Her knowledge of local species bordered on the encyclopedic. Before they'd met, Miles wouldn't have known the difference between a tufted titmouse and eastern phoebe if both were perched on his nose. But during the time he and Josie had spent together over the summer, he'd made a point of learning how to distinguish the two (the titmouse is a lighter shade of gray and has a rust-colored patch under its wings) and dozens of other species as well. He still couldn't identify birds by their songs the way Josie did, though. Baby steps.

"Sounds perfect," Miles said. And he meant it. What about an hour spent walking through the woods with Josie—the breeze sighing through her hair, her face lighting up at the distant sound of a woodpecker drumming against a tree—wouldn't be perfect?

Nothing is the answer. Nothing at all. Don't ask stupid questions.

Maybe his dad would let him off restrictions just this once. . . .

"Great!" Josie said. She started writing in her notebook, the bird-shaped cap eraser on the end of her pencil bouncing like a robin across the lawn. "Here's the pavilion number where the hike starts." She tore out the paper and passed it to Miles. "I'll pack us some snacks, too."

Miles slid the paper into the back pocket of his jeans. "Sounds perfect."

"You already said that, O ye of little words."

Miles shrugged. "I don't know another word for 'perfect.'"

Josie stroked her chin, accepting the challenge. "Impeccable. Flawless. Pristine . . ." She rattled off the adjectives, oblivious that in the eyes of Miles—and anyone else with eyes that could see—she was describing herself.

"Okay, Ms. Thesaurus." Miles laughed. "Thanks for the vocab lesson."

"Just trying to help."

They sat quietly, looking at each other across the table. Josie smiled prettily because there was no other way for her to do it. Miles smiled goofily for the exact same reason. It was the kind of moment Miles figured his dad was talking about whenever he said he'd give anything to be thirteen again.

Josie pushed the stray lock of hair behind her ear. "So, what're you reading?"

"This?" Miles said innocently, holding up the comic book for Josie to see. "It's the latest *Gilded Age*. Henry gave it to me. It's all about the Unnd attack."

Puzzled, Josie's expression tightened. "The what attack?"

Oops. The name of the alien race had never been reported, probably because nobody from the news—or the rest of Earth, for that matter—spoke lizard-monster. The cape had translated their spitting, guttural language for Miles as he fought them, which was how he knew their true name.

"Did you say the 'Unnd' attack?"

Miles pretended to be puzzled right back. "What's an 'Unnd'?"

"I don't know. You're the one who said it."

"I said the *alien* attack," Miles enunciated. Then he pointed at his mouth. "Sometimes it's tough to hear each other with all the whispering."

Josie's eyes narrowed. "Is there something you're not telling me?"

Miles's resistance withered. Josie's gaze was more intense than a TV lawyer's—and TV lawyers always got their witnesses to spill the truth.

Why not just tell her about the cape? Three out of seven-plus billion was still a pretty good average. Josie may have been spending time with Miles, but imagine how much more she'd be into him if she knew who he really was.

Surely she'd seen the way other kids looked at them when they were together. It was always a look that said, *What's she doing with that nobody?* How much longer would it be before Josie started asking that question herself? All Miles had to do was say the words and Josie would understand exactly what she was doing with him. He wanted to say them—oh, how badly he wanted to. But then he caught a glimpse of Henry, and the temptation dissipated.

"Henry!" he yelled.

Mrs. Binding glared at Miles from behind her desk like she was trying to fry him with laser beams from her eyes. "Quiet."

"Sorry, Mrs. Binding," Miles called to her.

Mrs. Binding glared harder.

"I mean 'sorry,'" Miles whispered. "Again."

Henry took a seat with Miles and Josie. He tutored during fifth-period study hall, offering help to students who needed it. "What's up? Need me to go over your algebra assignment?"

"Hi, Henry," Josie said.

Henry looked at Josie as though just noticing her for the first time. He and Josie had lived on the same street since they were born, so they'd grown up together. Spending his life around her had somehow made him impervious to her charms. Just another item on the long list of his odd qualities. "Oh. Hey, Josie."

"Josie was just asking about this copy of *Gilded Age* you gave me."

"That?" Henry feigned nonchalance. "I've read better issues."

"Really?" Miles said, locking eyes with Henry. "I think it's pretty great."

Henry locked eyes in return. "It's not *that* great."

"You sure about that?" Miles said, opening up the comic book and pointing to one of the pages in the final, climactic scene against Lord Commander Calamity. "Gilded broke that big Unn—" Miles caught himself before slipping up in front of Josie again. "Er, *alien*'s weapon in half. Have you ever done anything like that, Henry?"

Henry huffed and adjusted his glasses. "Of course not. I'm not a superhero."

"That's right. You're not. So stop acting like you know anything about it."

Henry's mouth dropped open. He looked as though Miles has rolled up the copy of *Gilded Age* and swatted him across the nose with it.

Miles and Henry stared each other down in uncomfortable silence. Uncomfortable for everyone except Mrs. Binding, who probably wished it'd last until kingdom come.

Josie finally broke the stalemate. "What's the matter with you two? You become not-friends when I wasn't looking?" She reached for the copy of *Gilded Age*. "All this over a silly comic book?"

"It's not silly!" Miles barked, jerking the comic away from her.

"Quiet," Mrs. Binding reiterated. She punctuated her words with a fresh, laser-beam glare. "Second and final warning." Then she stood from her desk and steered her book-laden cart off into the stacks.

Josie crossed her arms and staked Miles to his seat with her stare. "Don't yell at me," she said, icicles hanging from her every word.

Miles looked away. He'd confused Josie on

occasion. He'd acted like a dork around her plenty. But this was the first time he'd made her angry. "Sorry."

Miles turned to Henry. "I don't know what made me say that, Henry. I'm sorry to you, too."

"Same here. I apologize. You know how I get about Gilded." Henry grinned slyly, knowing Josie would think he was talking as a fan of Gilded, not his collaborator.

"Anyway," Miles said, closing the comic book. "It's a good issue. But we can talk about it some other—"

"Whatcha reading, Taylor?" a voice boomed snidely.

Miles felt the blood drain from his face. Whenever he was suffering through a bad situation, there was always one person who arrived to make it worse.

"You take a wrong turn, Craig?" Henry said. "That word over the door spelled 'library,' not 'locker room.'"

Craig ignored Henry. "Just wanted to see what you twerps were reading." He dropped a hand on the copy of *Gilded Age*, crumpling it like it was the opposing team's playbook.

Miles bolted up from his chair. "Don't touch that!" he demanded.

Craig planted another hand in Miles's chest and shoved him back down in his seat.

"Relax. I'm just looking." Craig swatted through the pages, his thick fingers crinkling them. His hands were built for throwing running backs to the ground by their jerseys. Delicacy was a foreign language to them.

Miles seethed. "There are a lot of words there, Craig. You'll probably understand it better if you concentrate on the pictures."

Dude the Teammate rolled his eyes and exhaled deeply. "Dude." It was an honest expression of disbelief, as though Miles were down 63–0 and still thought he could win by running the ball up the middle.

Craig flexed a fist, his knuckles cracking like a lit pack of Black Cat fireworks. He looked like he was about to punch Miles's head clean off his shoulders. Which would be a completely realistic outcome for their confrontation.

"Leave him alone, Craig," Josie said.

Craig ignored her. He adjusted his weight on his legs, getting in tune with whatever primal energy source allowed him to hit with both speed and power. Miles suddenly understood how it must feel to line up across from the Jammer, praying to God and anyone else who'll listen that the quarterback forgets to call "hike." Where was Mrs. Binding when he needed her?

"Know what the difference between you and me is, Taylor?"

"About forty IQ points?" Henry chimed in.

Craig reached down and snatched Miles by the

front of his shirt, pulling him to a tiptoed position, so his sneakers just barely touched the floor. "The difference between you and me is that I'm good at something. No, forget that. I'm *great* at something. People talk about me. Newspapers print stories about me. Fans scream their heads off for me. But you? You'll never know what that's like." Craig held the comic book close to Miles's face. "All you'll ever be able to do is read about it."

Craig tossed Miles aside like he was made of paper. Like he was garbage. Miles skidded across the top of the table and would've plowed into Josie, if her reflexes hadn't been quick enough to get her clear. He landed hard on the floor, the air fleeing from his lungs like it had someplace to be in a hurry.

"Miles! Don't get up!" Josie hovered over him.

Miles glimpsed himself reflected in her dark eyes, and he hated what he saw. He sprang to his feet and charged. Ears burning and temper boiling, he ran at Craig with every ounce of speed and strength he could muster.

And then he was going in the opposite direction, his jaw stinging at the place where Craig had connected with his cinder-block fist. It'd happened so fast, Miles didn't realize he might get decked until he already had been. He toppled backward and smacked into a bookshelf. A copy of *Atlas of the World: 23rd*

Edition teetered forward and hit the floor. The sound echoed off the walls of the quiet room.

Miles dropped to his knees, cradling his jaw in both hands. A current of pain shot through his face. The fight went out of him, which was too bad for Craig because he appeared to be just getting started. He strode toward Miles like an attack dog who'd been let off the chain and was going to devour Miles's face, body, and self-esteem.

"Dude! Dude! Dude!" Dude the Teammate tugged frantically on Craig's arm, his eyes wide at the sight of Mrs. Binding's cart emerging from the stacks.

Craig turned his back on Miles and straightened up.

Mrs. Binding marched out from between the shelves of books, her footsteps somehow not making a single audible sound. She was like a stealth helicopter, rigged for silent running.

"What's all the commotion?" she said, her eyes scanning for a target.

"Nothing, Mrs. Binding," Craig answered in a hushed tone. "Taylor tripped going back to his chair." Craig bent down and reached out a hand toward Miles.

"That's a lie!" Josie blurted. "Craig—"

"Was just trying to help me back up," Miles cut in. Refusing Craig's hand, he stood on his own. "Just an accident, Mrs. Binding."

Miles could tell Mrs. Binding wasn't fooled. As much as he wanted to, he couldn't bring himself to tell her the truth. Saying aloud what had happened would make it ten times more real and permanent. Once he admitted it, it'd never go away.

Mrs. Binding pointed a no-nonsense finger at Craig. "Move along to your seat, Mr. Logg."

"Yes, ma'am." His back turned to Mrs. Binding, Craig held out the copy of *Gilded Age*, clenching his fist to crumple it one last time before dropping it on the table in front of Miles. "Thanks for the loan, Taylor. If you like seeing amazing feats, come to the game Friday."

Craig sauntered off, Dude the Teammate following after him.

CHAPTER 8

IT WAS THE WAY THE JAMMER TREATED MILES. Decking him. Humiliating him. Acting like Miles was a nobody. Because when he wasn't wearing the cape, Miles *was* a nobody.

There it was. As much as Miles hated—really, truly hated—admitting he'd learned something from the monolith of football and density that was Craig Logg, there was no denying it. In front of everyone in study hall, and Henry and Josie (worst of all, Josie), Craig had proved beyond a doubt what Miles was.

Miles couldn't even be mad about it. That'd be like water being mad because someone explained that it was wet—the water should've known that from the outset. Mostly Miles just felt stupid for believing he could ever be somebody.

All the news stories? They were about Gilded.

All the people Miles had seen wave at him as he'd

flown overhead? They were waving at Gilded.

The little boy Miles had pulled from the cabin of a boat sinking on Lake Lanier last Saturday? It was Gilded he'd hugged for diving to the bottom and retrieving his stuffed giraffe.

Gilded went out of his way to rescue stuffed animals. What was not to love about the guy?

But Miles Taylor? There was plenty not to love about him. If you even bothered to notice him. Saying kids like Miles were as common as leaves on trees would be an insult to greenery. At least every leaf on a tree is unique.

Had Henry been friends with Miles before the cape was in the picture? Nope. Was Mr. Taylor ever as proud of his son as every time he saw him leave their apartment as Gilded? Negative. Not even Miles's own mother had bothered to stick around.

Miles left study hall anxious for Henry to text him with a mission—any reason to be Gilded, even if for only a little while. Then he waited some more. By the time he was halfway through last-period language arts, he couldn't take it anymore. It had been *three days.* Three days isn't much time when your science project is due, but if it's time spent walking instead of flying, sitting instead of saving, it's an eternity.

Miles felt like he was suffocating, locked in a cage so small, the bars wouldn't allow him to breathe.

He had to get out. He had to be not-nobody.

He raised his hand.

Mrs. Denouement paused her reading of Shakespeare and looked excitedly at Miles. "Do you wish to make a comment, Miles?"

A comment? Miles had been so lost in his own misery, he didn't even know which play she was reading. Even if he did, Shakespeare's "thines" and "thous" were too confusing for him to understand. "Can I p-please be excused?" he asked shakily.

Mrs. Denouement raised her eyebrows in concern. She must've heard the quaver in Miles's voice, noticed the tremble in his raised hand. "Are you all right?"

"I just . . . I don't feel so good."

"*Well*, Miles. You don't feel *well*." Apparently, concern didn't prevent Mrs. Denouement from demanding adherence to proper grammar.

"Well," Miles echoed. "I don't feel well. I . . ."

Mrs. Denouement was nice. He didn't want to lie to her. But if he sat still one moment longer, he was going to scream. "I think I'm coming down with a fever."

Mrs. Denouement glanced at the wall clock. She scribbled down a hall pass and held it out for Miles. "Go see the nurse. Class is nearly dismissed, so you may take your belongings with you."

Miles snatched up his backpack and hurried toward the front of the class. Then he remembered he was supposed to be experiencing a bout of under-the-weather and he slowed his gait.

"Feel better," Mrs. Denouement said, smiling encouragingly.

Miles took the hall pass and headed out the door.

The halls were empty, but in a few minutes school would let out for the day and Miles would be overrun. Not to mention Henry would track him down and launch into another one of his strategy sessions dictating what Miles was and wasn't supposed to do.

He needed to move fast. He ducked into an alcove and began checking the local news apps on his phone.

The lead story on Fox 5 was about a local animal shelter's annual fund-raising dog-and-cat fashion show. Cute, but not an emergency by anyone's definition.

The top headline in the newsfeed for the *Atlanta Journal-Constitution* read LOCAL RESTAURANT FINED FOR COCKROACH INFESTATION. Gross—Miles now had an actual upset stomach to accompany his pretend fever—but not exactly the sort of event that justified superhero intervention.

All the news apps were the same. Human-interest stories or petty scandals. Miles had lied his way out of class and into the driest news drought ever. How does a hero pass the time when his city is getting along just fine all on its own?

Then Miles spotted it. A little tab in the upper-right corner of the app he was scrolling through: NATIONAL NEWS.

How was it fair that Atlanta was the only city in the world with a hometown superhero? Miles understood that his first priority was to keep his city safe. It made perfect sense. But that wasn't supposed to be his *only* priority, was it? It was a big world, its dangers even bigger. Gilded was powerful enough to handle them all. So why shouldn't he?

Miles put himself in the shoes of a thirteen-year-old kid from, well, anywhere that wasn't Atlanta. Houston, Orlando, Charlotte . . . it didn't matter. How would it feel to grow up in one of those places, to be bombarded by news of fires and natural disasters and crimes and know there was a superhero in the world who could help if he chose to, but never, ever did?

Miles couldn't relate. He'd been born and raised in Atlanta, and he'd never journeyed far from home. Gilded had been a constant in his life, a bright, shining reminder that there wasn't anything to be afraid of.

How did the saying go? Think local, act global. (Or was it the other way around? Eh, that wasn't important anyway.)

Miles tapped the tab and launched himself into the news of the nation.

Whoa.

There was a lot of stuff happening.

Headlines filled the screen. One in particular leaped out at him: ALERT ISSUED FOR MISSING NASHVILLE GIRL. A six-year-old had gone missing from her neighbor's backyard. She had bad asthma, and her mother was pleading for everyone to help locate her because she was already past the time when she was supposed to take her medicine.

What could be worse than a little girl not being able to find her parents and her parents not even knowing where to look for her? And here Miles was, safe inside a school building doing absolutely zero about it.

One thing was for sure—nothing was ever going to get done so long as Miles was standing around thinking. Any second now the bell would ring and the halls would be too clogged for him—Gilded—to sprint through. He had to move now.

Miles tossed his phone into his backpack and pulled out the cape. It hummed, its golden light setting Miles's face aglow.

So what if Craig could tackle kids on a football field? Big deal. How many eighth graders were good at sports? A thousand? A million?

And what did it matter that his dad had him on restrictions? This was serious business. Superhero business. Was Miles really expected to care about middle school when there were so many more important things he could be doing?

Miles was one of a kind. He wasn't a nobody. He was the ultimate somebody. All he had to do was put on the cape and show everyone who wanted to hold him back what true excellence was.

The cape flickered and went dark.

Miles rubbed it. He shook it. He tried pushing the clasp halves together and making them stick.

And then he got scared. Really scared. You-feel-like-you're-going-to-cry-because-you're-so-desperate-and-you-don't-know-what-to-do-now scared. A-kid-might-get-hurt-and-maybe-even-die-if-he-didn't-find-a-way-to-help scared.

Miles thought of the people who needed him right now. A terrified little girl so short of breath she couldn't even yell for her parents. Her mom clutching an inhaler, praying for her child's safe return.

The cape vibrated awake, sending pulses of energy like drumbeats through his body. It shone in a dazzling burst, reflecting off the walls of the alcove.

No need to push the clasp halves together now. They leaped together all on their own.

Gilded was going to answer the nation's call.

Where the heck was Nashville, anyway?

NASHVILLE...
NASHVILLE...

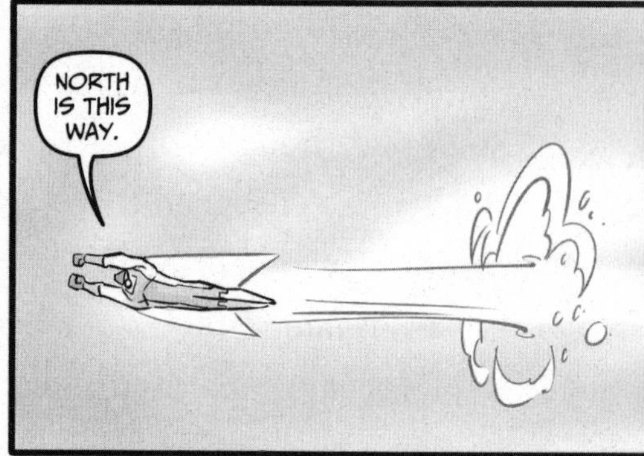
NORTH IS THIS WAY.

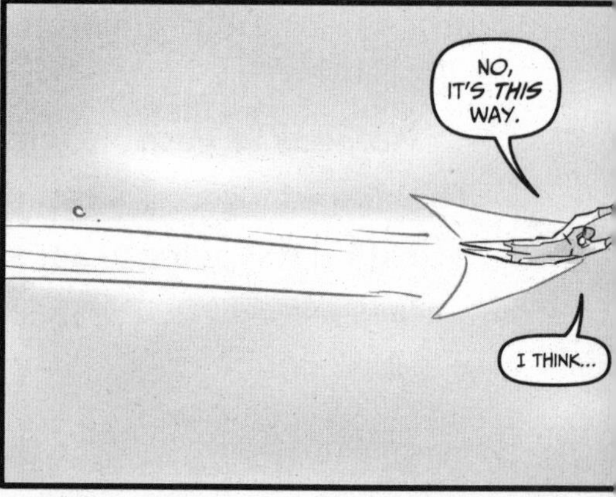
NO, IT'S *THIS* WAY.
I THINK...

ID READY
AUG.
TUES.
MAN VS MACHINE
Road ATLAS

DING DING!
OPEN

EXCUSE ME?
HM?
MAN VS MACHINE
ARE ROBOTS TAKING OUR JOBS

COULD YOU, LIKE, TELL ME HOW TO GET TO NASHVILLE?

HERE. BORROW A ROAD ATLAS.
Road ATLAS
YOU SURE?

THANKS!

SNIFF
THOUGHT I KNEW THE WAY.

DON'T BE SCARED, KID.
MOMMY AND DADDY SAY NOT TO TALK TO STRANGERS.
SNIFF

STRANGER? *EVERYBODY* KNOWS ME.

YOU...
YOU'RE...

YEP. I'M GILDED.
I WAS GONNA SAY... *FLYING*.

I USED MY SUPER-EYESIGHT TO SPOT YOU WHEN I WAS UP THERE.
WANT TO JOIN ME? WE CAN SEE WHAT YOUR HOUSE LOOKS LIKE FROM THE SKY.

IT'S OKAY. YOU CAN LOOK. I WON'T DROP YOU.
PROMISE?
PROMISE.

I'M A *SUPERHERO*.

87%
Alert Issued for Missing Nashville Girl
MOMMY! DADDY! LOOK WHO I FOUND!

The little girl had laughed and screamed with delight all the way home, like Gilded was the best carnival ride she'd ever been on. Her parents had thanked him so much, Miles thought they were going to ask him inside for dinner. Sure, the whole thing had started out scary, but now they had a story they could tell for the rest of the lives. They'd met Gilded. Lucky them.

And Miles had a story of his own. Here he was in Nashville, sitting in a park along the bank of the Cumberland River, the cape stowed safely in his backpack again. The dark water wound past him, glittering in the afternoon sun. Picnickers lounged on blankets. Shoppers browsed the rows of trendy stores behind him. Miles had been tubing on the Chattahoochee plenty of times, but that always seemed more like a wilderness trip—mud and bugs and getting stuck in shallow water.

That all felt a million miles away. You know what else felt a million miles away? Mr. Taylor's restrictions, Henry's lectures, and the Jammer and his stupid bullying. All the things that made Miles feel small had been left back home like a great, big heap of trash waiting at the curb.

Home. Miles had been gone a couple of hours. He might be able to make it back before Henry or Mr. Taylor caught on he was gone. Not that it mattered. Word was sure to spread that Gilded has been to Nashville. It wouldn't be long before that news made it back to the radio and TV stations in Atlanta. There was no avoiding that, sooner or later, Miles would be forced to face up to a Nashville-sized breaking of the rules.

Between sooner or later, later sounded better. Way better.

Miles checked the news apps again. In Chicago, a loaded cement truck had collided with one of the pillars beneath a highway overpass, and the overpass was on the verge of collapsing. Repair crews needed to get to work, but they were worried the bridge was going to come down on top of them.

Forget Mr. Taylor and Henry. Good-bye rules and procedures. Just thinking about them made Miles angry. Who were they to tell him what to do? He was Gilded, and people needed him. School and bedtime were for nobodies, not superheroes. Miles was headed to Chicago. After that . . . well, he'd just have to check his phone and see.

There were a lot of people in the park, but none of them were paying any attention to Miles. Why would they? He was just an average kid with a backpack. Nothing special at all.

Not anymore. Never again.

Miles slipped out the cape and settled it onto his shoulders. An overpass. He'd never lifted one of those before. Next stop—

76%
Chicago Highway
Overpass Threatens
Collapse

DON'T WORRY!
HNNF
I CAN HOLD IT!

HOLLYWOOD FIRE DEPT
YOU'RE PROBABLY WONDERING WHY I'M NOT USING A ***WATER TOWER.*** SEE, THERE'S THIS THING CALLED HYDROSTATIC PRESSURE...

68%
Wildfire Spreads to Los Angeles Hills

HERE'S THE BAD GUY YOU'RE LOOKING FOR, OFFICERS.
N. HOUSTON St.
59%
Armed Robber Terrorizes Dallas Businesses

WEST END MARKETPLACE
CINEM
DALLAS
POLIC

51%
Mountain Lion
Stalks Denver
Suburbs

ROWR?!
GOOD KITTY. AWAY FROM THE CITY YOU GO.

TUES
TRAVELS THROUGH TIME
Road ATLAS
GO FISH
THANKS FOR THE LOAN!

Miles had completed a whirlwind tour, crisscrossing the United States from south to north and east to west. It was all a blur, like the scenery he passed over while flying at super-speed. It's a good thing Gilded was already bald because wind resistance at infinity miles per hour would've stripped the hair right off his head.

The best Miles could piece it together, he'd seen a sunset and a sunrise while he was gone. Now here he was back at Chapman, watching kids exit their buses and file into the building to start the school day. He'd accomplished a lot in the last twenty-four hours, but he'd missed dinner, bedtime, and breakfast.

Yikes.

When he thought about it like that, it sounded like such a long time. While he was in the thick of it, it'd all gone by so fast. Sure, he'd paused once or twice to consider whether he should return home. But he knew his dad and Henry would be furious about him going off on his own again and—

vrrrrrrr

vrrrrrrr

vrrrrrrr

vrrrrrrr

vrrrrrrr

Miles's pocket erupted in a fit of vibration. It felt like there were a dozen windup toys in his pants and they'd decided to have a war. He dug out his cell phone and checked the screen.

Forty-three missed calls, plus one hundred twenty-seven waiting text messages.

Double yikes.

Miles had ignored the messages he noticed while checking his phone between cities. He could only imagine how angry his dad was, seeing news stories about Gilded—Miles—popping up in Dallas and Los Angeles, and not being able to reach him.

You know what? Miles was angry right back. He didn't need a babysitter. What did his dad have to be worried about? He knew Miles was safe. All he had to do was turn on the TV and he'd see what Miles had been up to. Besides, Miles couldn't be not safe. He was in-freaking-vincible. Or at least Gilded was. Which was the same thing, right? Right.

As he folded the cape and returned it to his backpack, Miles suddenly realized he was dog-tired. The cape had kept him energized while he was wearing it, but as he walked toward the bus corral, it took a concerted effort just to put one foot in front of the other, like he was trudging through wet cement. He yawned, grinding his fists into his fog-covered eyes.

School. What was the point? After every amazing thing he'd done the past two days, Miles was supposed to sit through class lectures like all the other kids? Forget it. His dad would be at work, meaning there'd be nothing waiting for him at the apartment except the food in the fridge and his nice, soft bed.

A long sleep. That was exactly what he needed. It'd help him clear his head and regain his strength for the argument with his dad that he knew was going to happen. It *had* to happen. Time for *him* to establish the boundaries of being Gilded.

Plus, there was Henry. Miles absolutely did not need another sermon about all the ways he'd violated the procedures. He imagined Henry pacing around the bus corral like an Old West lawman waiting for a fugitive to step off a train. His smartphone would be drawn and fully loaded with data.

No way. Miles was too sleep deprived to put up with that. Skipping school was a much better plan.

Miles turned and headed back in the direction he'd come from.

"*Mis*-ter *Tay*-lor!" a voice boomed, with stern emphasis placed on the first syllable in each word.

Miles stopped dead. He turned and saw Assistant Principal Harangue standing behind him with his brown-bag lunch clutched in one fist. He was no doubt looking forward to beginning another day of doling out detentions, but Miles couldn't tell by his stone-faced expression. "Care to explain why you've wandered so far from your bus? Are you lost, or did you forget what the school building looks like?"

"No, Mr. Harangue," Miles answered. Then he thought again. "I mean, yes, Mr. Harangue. I mean . . . Which question should I answer first?"

Mr. Harangue jabbed a thick finger at the school, like he was pinning it to the landscape. "Move."

So much for sleep. As for avoiding Henry, Miles would have to bang on the side door until someone let him in. If he went through the main entrance, he was toast.

Miles bowed his head and dragged himself toward the building.

CHAPTER 9

MILES COLLAPSED INTO HIS DESK LIKE HIS batteries had died. Mr. Essaye wouldn't start class for a few minutes, which sounded to Miles like a few more minutes of sleep than he'd had the night before. He folded his arms into a pillow and laid down his head.

Josie had once told him about the albatross, a type of bird that could fly all the way around the world without touching land once. Miles couldn't fathom how draining that amount of exertion would be.

Until now.

"Miles?" Josie leaned over in her desk. "Are you sure you're okay to be at school?"

"What makes you think I'm not okay?" Miles said, yawning.

"You just don't look too . . . with it, is all."

"I'm fine. I just stayed up late last night. Is that a crime?"

Josie pulled back. That last bit had come out

harsher than Miles had meant it to, but he wasn't in the mood to be interrogated.

"Look," Josie said sternly. "I don't know what your problem is, but last time we talked, we made plans to go on a bird hike. I waited for you more than an hour. I missed the hike completely, which is too bad because I heard they spotted a Bachman's sparrow. You know how rare that is this far north?"

The bird hike. Miles had forgotten all about his plans with Josie. Flying off to save the world was one thing, but the least he could've done was give Josie a call. Actually, the least he could've done was text her. But he'd neglected even to do that.

"Josie, I should've let you know I wasn't going to make it. I'm sorry."

Josie frowned. "So you weren't sick?"

"No."

"Then why'd you stand me up?"

"Um . . ." Miles had to think fast. Much faster than his sleep-starved brain was presently capable of. "I don't remember."

"Oh, well," Josie huffed. "That's a relief. I was worried you might've ditched me for something important."

"It was important!" Miles blurted.

"But you don't remember what it was?"

"Yes!"

Josie furrowed her brow. "You *do* remember?"

"No!"

"Make up your mind," Josie said, exasperated.

Miles wanted to put his head down, pass out, and wake up when all of this was over. He mustered what little brainpower he had left. "I can explain."

The classroom door opened, and in stepped Henry. He leveled a stare at Miles like his eyes were the sun, his glasses were the magnifying glass, and Miles was the ant.

Uh-oh.

Henry handed Mr. Essaye a hall pass. Mr. Essaye read it, then looked at Miles.

"Miles, gather your things. You're wanted in Assistant Principal Harangue's office."

Miles grabbed his backpack and walked to the front of the room. The class was silent, every kid watching him with the intensity of a crowd witnessing a criminal walking to the gallows.

Miles looked back over his shoulder at Josie, who was pretending to study something in her notebook. She wasn't wrong—Miles had treated her poorly. As his dad would say, Taylors were raised better than that. But being Gilded was all that mattered. There were activities in the world more important than bird hikes. If only he could tell her.

Miles stopped in front of Henry. "What's up?"

Henry was deadpan. "Follow me." Henry exited the room with Miles in tow.

"I'm really tired, Henry," Miles said, as the classroom door closed behind them. "Whatever this is about, let's talk about it later."

Henry wheeled on Miles, eyes shooting double-edge swords. "Do you think I'm an idiot? Stop acting like you don't know what this is about." Henry's voiced cracked, his anger shattering his words.

Maybe it was fatigue from the all-nighter Miles had just pulled. Maybe all the little things—Henry criticizing his performance all the time, or telling him where he should and shouldn't go and when—had finally gathered into a single big thing too large to ignore. Maybe he was just cranky. Whatever the reason, Miles wasn't going to take it anymore.

"Whatever," Miles snapped. "This is about me going it alone, isn't it? You know what? You're not my boss. You're here to help me use my powers to help others. And that's what I did. You're just mad I didn't include you."

Henry's eyes narrowed. "Is that what I'm mad about?" He rested his hand on his smartphone's holster. It was like he was daring Miles to push him further.

"Here we go with the phone!" Miles blurted, throwing his hands up in a show of aggravation. "What is it this time? The Gilded Group members are upset I went to other cities? Too bad. I don't work for them, either. Who are they to tell me I can't spend some nights spreading the heroism around?"

Henry wrinkled his nose. "Spreading the heroism around? You sound like you plan to do more of that."

Miles could see where this conversation was headed. If Henry thought Miles's trip had been a one-time thing, then he'd probably let it slide. But Miles wasn't in a let-it-slide mood. He was in a hold-his-ground, no-one-was-going-to-order-him-around mood.

"Why shouldn't I? It's a big world, you know. It's full of people who need my help."

"Your help," Henry stated.

"That's what I said."

"Not Gilded's?"

"Same thing."

"No, Miles," Henry said icily. "It isn't. You're an eighth grader. Gilded is a superhero. If you're having trouble remembering who's who, you're the one with the zits."

Miles's jaw tightened. "Watch it, Henry. Now isn't a good time to take cheap shots."

Henry sighed, knitting his brow like a concerned mother. "You're right. You're a wreck. You won't be any good to anyone today." He reached into his shoulder bag, pulling out a pad of nurse's slips and a pen.

"I'm signing you out," he said, scribbling. "Go home and get some sleep."

Sleeeeep.

Miles mustered enough energy to smile. "Finally, something we agree on."

Henry scowled, then ripped the slip from the pad. "Here's something we aren't going to agree on. Hand over the backpack."

Miles jolted like he'd been doused with ice water. "What?"

Henry held out his hand. "You heard me. I'm grounding you. Give me the cape."

Miles stepped away from Henry, his fingers clenching the straps of his backpack. It was instinct. He was protecting what was his and his alone. "No."

Henry took on the posture of a ten-foot-tall man packaged inside a below-five-foot-tall body. He meant business. "You can't be trusted with it. I let you leave here with it, you won't go home. You'll go searching for a fender bender or a cat stuck in a tree—any excuse to turn into Gilded.

"It's only for a few hours. Just long enough for you to get some rest. We'll talk about it more when you have a clear head."

Miles's head was abundantly clear. He pressed his back against the wall of the hallway. "No," he repeated.

Henry stepped forward, staring up into Miles's

face. He pushed his glasses up his nose, which for Henry was the equivalent a barroom brawler rolling up his sleeves before a fistfight.

"Miles, you *will* give me that cape, or I *won't* give you a slip to go home. I'll go to Mr. Harangue and tell him I caught you cutting class. I'll tell him I suspect you have contraband in your backpack. He'll take it from you. He'll search it. What do you think will happen then?"

There was no telling what would happen then. Mr. Harangue probably wouldn't think anything of the cape, except that Miles was a little too old to be bringing a superhero costume to school.

But what if he thought more? What if the cape was vibrating? What if he caught a glimpse of its beautiful, enthralling glow? He might get scared and turn it over to the police. He might keep it for himself. Whatever happened, it'd be the end. Miles would go back to being a nobody. Forever.

Miles's resolve weakened. "You wouldn't."

Henry lifted onto his tiptoes and craned his neck upward, almost bringing his eyes directly in line with Miles's. "Try me."

Miles wilted. All the incredible things he's done over the past two days, but he was powerless to defend himself against a pint-sized kid threatening to tattletale. He was embarrassed and infuriated, the heat of both burning his skin. He shrugged off his backpack and shoved it at Henry. "Here."

Henry nodded. "You're doing the right thing."

Miles simmered. "What if something goes wrong, Henry? What if the world needs me?"

Henry pushed the nurse's slip into Miles's hand. "The world *does* need you. I know you don't believe me, but that's why I'm doing this. Go home. I'll meet you at your apartment after school. I won't let the cape out of my sight, I promise. As for the world, it can survive a few hours without you."

Henry walked off, Miles's backpack clutched to his chest.

Miles wanted to run after him, beg him to give back the cape, swear to be better. But he knew it was no use. Henry had made up his mind. Miles was stuck being himself until Henry decided otherwise.

He'd never felt so small and alone.

CHAPTER 10

ATLANTA WAS BURNING.

The sky was black with smoke and ash. Miles didn't know if it was day or night. The ground shook beneath his feet, like the Earth itself was being wounded. Somewhere in the distance, a woman screamed.

Miles couldn't remember how he'd arrived downtown. He didn't know what caused the cataclysm. He only knew he had to stop it. He reached for his backpack, knowing the answer lay safely hidden within.

It was gone.

He searched the ground frantically for his backpack. Acrid haze seared his eyes, stopping him from seeing. It grew thicker, billowing over and around him. He choked and spluttered, wiping his face until soot-stained tears muddied his hands and cheeks.

A skyscraper crumbled. The ground shuddered anew. Another scream in the distance. "Gilded! Please, save us!"

Miles wanted to answer, but the smoke smothered his words. *I'm here!* he thought desperately. *Has anyone seen my backpack?*

Miles bolted upright in bed, his sheets sopped with sweat. Lightning flashed, setting his dark room aglow. A thunderclap followed on its heels, rolling through like an overburdened cargo train. Then came the hushed beats where the world takes stock.

A Georgia storm was in the offing.

It was night, but which night? Miles's extended stint as Gilded had caused him to completely lose track of time. Had he slept for hours? Days? He felt disconnected from the world, out of touch and out of sync. This, from a kid who hung his shirts in his closet arranged by color. All was not right in Miles Taylor's world.

Through the drowsiness, he heard voices murmuring in the living room: his dad and Henry. He couldn't make out their words, but he didn't need to. He knew what they were discussing.

He was awake now.

Miles leaped from his bed and pulled on his jeans and a T-shirt. This was a discussion he wouldn't allow himself to be excluded from. No way. The old man had given the cape to him. He alone knew how to wield it. And he would decide its future.

(Not until after he combed his hair and brushed his teeth, though. People with tangled hair and funky breath were never taken seriously.)

Miles threw open his bedroom door and strode down the hall. He was strong. He was confident. He was the Golden Great. And he was more than capable of knowing what was best for him.

Mr. Taylor and Henry were seated at the dinette table. They were hunched forward and talking close, like conspirators whispering in a foreign café.

"What's going on here?" Miles demanded.

Mr. Taylor sat back. His expression made it clear that only one person would be doing the demanding tonight, and it wasn't going to be Miles. He pointed in the direction of the living room sofa. "Sit. Down."

Strength, confidence, and greatness: evaporated.

"Yes, sir." Miles bowed his head and moved toward the sofa as instructed. You can be a thirteen-year-old. You can be a superhero. But when your dad looks at you like that, you do what the man says. The end.

"Dad, I—"

"Not one word," Mr. Taylor interrupted.

"Yes, sir."

Mr. Taylor and Henry followed Miles into the living room. Miles sat on the sofa, but they remained standing. Miles remembered a time when his dad was suspicious of Henry. When Henry and Miles were a team, working together to prevent Mr. Taylor and everyone else from finding out about the cape. Now Henry and Mr. Taylor were the "we," and Miles was the outsider. Forces were allying against him.

Then Miles saw it. Henry must've had it stashed somewhere out of sight before, but now he had the backpack—Miles's backpack—holding the cape—Miles's cape—over his shoulders. It looked awkward on him, too big and bulging for his small frame.

On Miles the backpack fit like Baby Bear's bed: just right. Because he was the hero. He saved people. He thwarted disasters.

Henry didn't know anything about that. All he did was sit around, face buried in his phone, and think up new things to scold Miles about.

Maybe sensing he was a lousy match for the backpack and its contents, Henry slipped it off and set it on the coffee table. Miles gauged whether he could snatch it up and be out the window before anyone stopped him. He'd slept the whole day and maybe longer, plenty of time for the world to fall into danger. He was definitely needed somewhere. Right now.

Miles reached into his pocket for his cell phone, but it was empty.

"Searching for this?" Mr. Taylor said, holding up the phone. "I'll be keeping it."

"You can't!" Miles protested.

Mr. Taylor fumed. "You were gone all night! No phone call home. No checking in to tell me you were okay. Henry thankfully had the good sense to let me know what was going on. I'm your dad, and the only way I knew what part of the country you were in was to hope somebody was covering it on the news. This has to stop, son. It *will* stop. In this household, if you break the rules, there are consequences." He slid the phone into the back pocket of his work pants. "Henry says you two can get along just fine without your phone. So that's how it's going to be. Welcome to consequences."

Henry nodded in agreement, like sticking the knife in Miles's back didn't warrant a second thought.

"Henry doesn't know anything!" Miles wasn't going to let them gang up on him. He was the sole inheritor of the cape. Everyone else was nonessential personnel. "So he carries a phone in a holster. Big deal. He just likes pretending he's in on the action."

"Pretending?" Henry spluttered. "*Pretending?*"

Mr. Taylor put a hand on Henry's shoulder. "I'll handle this." Then he turned to Miles, his expression resolute. "If taking away your phone has you this hot, you're really not going to like this next bit: I'm taking the cape, too."

"That's not fair!" Miles erupted. Take the cape? That was too insane to even consider. "That girl in Nashville and the gunman in Dallas—those weren't traffic jams. Those were real emergencies putting real people in danger. Was I supposed to ignore them? You're acting like you *want* people to get hurt."

"Don't you dare put that on me. You're Gilded. I know that. But, darn it, you're also my son. Taking care of you is my number one job. Everyone else . . . I hope they have their own people to look out for them. I really do. Because it can't always be you."

The backpack was within reach. Miles imagined the cape glowing inside, its gorgeous, golden light begging to be let out. No one but him could make it shine. "It *can* always be me," he said defiantly. "It *will* be."

Mr. Taylor raked his fingers through his hair, like he was going to rip it out by the roots. "What's the matter with you? It's gotten so I can't even talk sense to you."

Henry unzipped Miles's backpack and reached inside. Miles envisioned Henry's fingers probing for the cape, grabbing it roughly as though it were his to do with as he wished. His internal reaction was visceral, instinctual, like how he imagined a guard dog felt when an intruder started its way up a fence. It took everything he had not to jump at Henry, canines bared. Every. Thing.

What Henry pulled from the backpack wasn't the cape, but the copy of *Gilded Age* he'd gifted to Miles. "I bought this for you," he said, handing the comic book to Miles. "What do you think about when you see it?"

Miles rolled his eyes and snatched the copy from Henry. "You want me to give you a book report now? What's next, writing sentences on a dry-erase board?"

Miles glanced down at the cover image of Gilded's right cross punching the toothy snarl off Lord Commander Calamity's face. The image thrilled him just as it had the first time he'd seen it—and every time he'd thought of it since.

"I see *me*," Miles said, emphasizing the "me" so that it also implied "not you." He flipped the comic book onto the coffee table.

Henry pressed his lips together. Miles was getting under his skin. Good. This was a waste of time, particularly to the people of the world who needed Gilded right now. The sooner it was over, the better.

Henry picked the comic book up again and began flipping through the pages. "Sure," he hissed. "Of course you see *you*. But I don't. I see a hero who was scared to death but risked his life anyway because he knew he had to. Not because he wanted to be on the cover of a comic book but because it was the right thing to do. That's not you anymore. At least not right now. Right now you're a whiny eighth grader who thinks decking a few aliens means he has the brainpower to be global guardian."

Ouch. So it was going to be like that? Fine. Let it be like that.

"At least I can't be replaced by a smartphone," Miles said.

"Son," Mr. Taylor cut in, "Henry has been a friend to you. You best stop and think about what kind of friend you want to be back to him."

Henry looked at Mr. Taylor. Miles could tell he'd cut him deep. "I'm fine, Mr. Taylor. I can hack it."

Henry turned the backpack over, emptying the contents onto the coffee table. Miles's math book and a couple of pencils tumbled out, the flowing fabric of the cape sliding after. It was a treasure, and Henry had dumped it onto the table like sweaty gym socks. Where was the respect?

"Remember how we met?" Henry said. "You'd just gotten the cape. You didn't know the first thing about how to use it. Sometimes it worked for you and sometimes it didn't, and you had no clue why. We figured it out together. It only works when you do what's right.

"Think about how amazing that is. All the heroes we look up to, but we always get let down in the end. Remember the baseball player who got caught gambling on his own games? And then there was that teen actress who always plays nice girls in the movies, but got videoed at the mall being mean to her own mom. Turned out they were both just people. We all do bad stuff sometimes.

"But not Gilded. He can't be bad. He can't ever do

wrong. He's the totally perfect hero who makes us all want to be better people. And he'll never disappoint us."

It could've been a reflection on his glasses, but Miles thought he saw a hint of tears welling at the bottoms of Henry's eyes.

"Things are really hard for you right now," Henry continued. "You've got responsibilities coming at you from every direction, and you don't know what to do. I blame myself. I should've realized it was happening. I'm not sure what to do about it yet, but just like before, we'll figure it out. Together."

Miles saw the sincerity in Henry's demeanor. There was no faking something like that. He really did want to help.

Then the unthinkable happened.

Henry grabbed the cape.

He slid his fingers across the shimmering fabric, and he smiled. The cape glowed, its beautiful light reflecting off his face.

Miles knew how that light felt—warm like a spring sun—but he couldn't feel it right then. He couldn't hear the soothing hum. But he bet Henry felt and heard it all.

How had Miles not seen this coming? It was so obvious now.

"You're jealous," Miles breathed.

Henry's head snapped around. "What?"

"I'm so stupid. You want the cape. *You* want to be Gilded. That's what this has been about the whole time. Telling me what to do and where to go. Deciding when I can wear the cape and when I can't. You want me to fail. So you can convince everyone you deserve the cape instead of me."

"You're stupid all right," Henry said angrily. He stood from the sofa, the cape clenched in one fist.

"And you," Miles said, glaring at his dad. "You don't like me being Gilded, either. You liked it better when I was just me. The new kid in school with no friends. The kid whose own mother didn't want to be around him. Because then it was just us hanging out all the time. Well, I have more important things to do now."

Mr. Taylor looked at Miles like he was speaking a made-up language that made no sense. "I have no idea what to say. When did you stop being you?"

"Don't say anything. Just know that I'm onto you. *Both* of you. But I'm not going to give up being Gilded. Not ever. *I* am Gilded. Gilded is *me*. I'm a hero."

"You . . . you . . ." Henry was bubbling like a volcano about to explode. "You call yourself a HERO?"

Miles puffed his chest out, pride inflating him. "Everyone calls me a hero. All the people who've seen me fly. All the readers of *Gilded Age*. Anyone who watches the news or listens to the stories about me on the radio. That's who calls me a hero."

Henry looked so mad, if his ears were steam whistles, they would've been shrieking. "They're wrong. Maybe you were once, but now I'm not sure. If you were a true hero, the best day of your life would be the day you didn't have to wear the cape anymore. The day the world didn't need Gilded because no one was in danger or getting hurt.

"But you?" Henry jabbed his finger at Miles. "You *want* to wear the cape. You *want* to be a hero. Don't you get what that means? It means you *want* bad things to happen. You look forward to them. Because they give you a reason to be Gilded."

Miles balled his hands into fists. "You have no idea what you're talking about, so quit pretending you know anything about being a hero. Get it through your tiny head: You aren't Gilded."

"Clearly," Henry snapped. "But at least my tiny head has a brain in it."

Mr. Taylor stepped in. "That's about enough from the both of you. Henry makes a point, son. There's no denying it. More and more you search for reasons to go to the cape. Jackknifed chicken trucks and rush-hour traffic and all manner of other nuisances. It's like you're hogging all the heroism to yourself. At first I thought it was just your way, you trying to organize the world like your skivvies drawer. I guess that's why I wasn't as harsh with your punishment as I should've been when you broke your promise about dialing yourself back.

"But I won't make that mistake again. Now I see there's something else to it. It's gotten so it doesn't matter if Gilded is needed. It's about *you* wanting to be needed. It ain't right." He held his hand toward Henry. "Give me the cape."

Miles's head was pounding as though his heart knew it couldn't burst out through his chest and was trying to go the skull route instead. Henry and his dad were trying to take everything away from him. He couldn't allow it. Gilded—Miles—was too important.

Miles shot up from the sofa. Quicker than Henry or his dad could react, he snatched the cape. "I'M GILDED!"

"Miles! No!" Henry shouted.

A blinding shock of lightning cracked outside. Thunder rattled the building. Miles didn't care. He dashed for the window, dropping the cape over his shoulders as he moved.

"Stop!" Mr. Taylor yelled.

Henry leaped onto Miles, but there was no tackling him. Miles concentrated, imagining a world imperiled. Seismic upheaval. Dinosaurs brought back to life. It didn't matter what or why. All that mattered was that Gilded was flying to the world's aid.

KSSSH

MILES!

MILES! STOP!
UNFF
I WON'T LOSE MY BOY!

NO ONE WILL TAKE MY CAPE! NOT EVER!
MILES!
MILES TAYLOR IS USELESS. GONE.
WHERE ARE YOU?!
I'M GILDED. I'M A HERO!

MILES! YOU GET BACK HERE THIS *INSTANT*, YOUNG MAN!

HAHAHA!

AND IF I *DON'T*? ARE YOU GOING TO *GROUND* ME? I'M--

MILES! YOU'RE IN DANGER!

I'M FALLING!

NOOOOOO!

The cape was silent. Inert.

All Miles wanted was to be Gilded.

The

cape

blinked

out

again.

Miles

couldn't

hold

on

anymore.

WHOOOOM

Miles had crashed down in an overgrown field behind a half-vacant strip mall. He was disoriented, on his back in the trench his impact had carved into the soggy ground. He wasn't hurt, but he was wet and cold, the fat drops of windblown rain stinging his skin.

The storm was intensifying.

Miles sat up on his knees, clutching the cape tightly. It didn't glow. It didn't hum. The storm that battered his body was nothing compared to the storm raging inside him.

The cape was rejecting him.

"Miles! Where are you?"

He heard a faint voice call over the blustery wind. Through the rain, he spied a bouncing circle of light. It darted back and forth in search of him.

Miles couldn't let Henry or his dad see him like this. They'd say "I told you so." His dad would take the cape. Maybe never give it back.

Miles ran. Not toward home or friends. He ran away. Rain pelted his face. He didn't know which way he was going. He just kept running with the cape clutched in his muddy hand. He risked a look back over his shoulder and saw the circle of light was pointed right at him. Through the gloom, he could just make out Henry's vague shape behind the glare.

Miles ran faster, his legs burning from the effort to get anywhere he and the cape could never be separated.

His foot caught on a rock. He tumbled forward, landing facedown on the sodden earth, sliding through the muck and mud. He came up spitting grass and gritty water. The cape lay in a mud puddle next to him, dark as the rain-choked night.

"Miles!" Henry rushed over, examining Miles's state. "I saw you fall from the sky. I thought for sure you were dead. Are you hurt?"

It wasn't lost on Miles that Henry was in a thunderstorm with winds strong enough to turn him into the world's first human kite, but all he could think about was him.

"I'm all right." Miles held forward the lifeless cape. The next words he spoke were nearly too heavy for his voice to lift. "I think . . . I think I broke it."

Suddenly, the wind picked up even greater speed, thrashing water about like a cyclone.

"What's happening?" Miles could barely hear his voice over the noise.

Henry clung to Miles. "I don't know!"

Miles looked up just as a glaring, white spotlight shined down from overhead. If he hadn't already been using his hand to shield his eyes from the rain, he would've been blinded. Was it the Unnd? Had

Lord Commander Calamity somehow sensed that Gilded was out of commission and returned to finish the job?

The light descended. Miles wanted to run, but his feet were rooted in the mud sucking at his feet. The cape offered no response. All Miles could manage was to watch helplessly as the light dropped closer on its collision course with him. Now he knew how it felt to be a deer transfixed by headlights on a midnight country road.

The light banked hard, and Miles saw it wasn't beaming down from a spaceship at all. It came from a helicopter.

No. Not a helicopter. Helicopters were things tourists used to get a bird's-eye view of the city. This was a state-of-the-art weapon of war. Guns and missile launchers jutted from its sides like porcupine quills. Miles hadn't noticed it before because it was painted black to blend in with the dark sky. The engine was whisper-quiet, scarcely audible over the sound of the rain beating the ground.

Henry wiped his glasses to get a better look. "Oh, no," he breathed. "They found us."

The helicopter touched down. Several hulking, shadowy figures lurched from its sides. The light was shining right in Miles's eyes, so all he could see were their shapes. Most of them looked identical—tall, broad, and their right arms pointing some sort of gun. Actually, it looked like their right arms *were* guns, but that didn't make any sense. Miles must've knocked his head harder than he thought.

One of the figures was shorter and pudgier than the others, its movement more uneven. It stepped closer, allowing Miles to see he was a soldier of some kind.

"Put down the weapon!" the soldier ordered.

Miles threw his hands up in a gesture of surrender. The wind caught the cape and billowed it like a flag flapping in the breeze. "Weapon?" he screamed in panic and confusion. "We're eighth graders!"

Henry grabbed Miles's hand, lowering it. "He's talking about the cape, Miles. He wants you to put down the cape."

Just then two of the shadowy figures moved aside to allow a tall, thin figure dressed in combat fatigues to stride past. He had deep grooves in his face and a thick, white mustache sprouting from his lip. The wind and rain didn't seem to bother him, as though he were a chunk of granite who'd weathered far worse storms than this. Miles could swear he'd seen him before.

"Children?" The man scowled, like the word tasted bad on his tongue. Then he shrugged, as if it made no difference what age Miles and Henry were.

"Mechanized infantry, secure the cape. Then bag these two up. They're coming with us."

The shadowy figures closed in. Light reflected off their rain-slicked skin like it was armor.

Miles felt a pinprick stab the back of his neck, and everything went black.

CHAPTER 11

BLINDING WHITE WALLS.

A cold, stainless-steel table.

Horrible, misshapen figures paced at the edge of Miles's vision, disappearing and reappearing like sharks swimming in and out of shadows.

The world was distorted and fuzzy around the edges, as though he were viewing it through milk-soaked cloth. He was unconscious, then semi-conscious, then unconscious again, all his effort spent on lifting eyelids that weighed a thousand pounds each. A throbbing ache pounded in his head and ears.

The last thing he remembered was the sharp pin-prick on his neck. He tried to reach for the spot, but his arms wouldn't move.

Oh, no.

He was strapped down to the table, thick metal brackets squeezing his wrists, waist, and ankles. He blinked, and it felt like his eyes were closed for a year.

When they finally rolled open again, figures were looming over him.

He saw now why they were misshapen—they wore balloonish suits like scientists had in sci-fi movies to protect themselves from radiation and who knows what else. One of the figures raised a gloved hand holding a syringe.

Who are you? Leave me alone!

Miles's mind screamed those things, but his mouth wouldn't say them. His tongue clicked thick and dry in his mouth. "Luk a-nuh."

"Subject Two is waking up," one of the figures said. It was a woman's voice, soft and clinical. "Administer more sedative."

A warm sensation like liquefied clouds started in Miles's neck and soaked up into his face and head.

No! Please!

Then . . . nothing.

CHAPTER 12

CHILDREN?

General Breckenridge sat behind his polished oak desk in his office, filled to bursting with distaste. He'd never been fond of children. Even when he was a child himself, he hadn't cared for the other children around him. He'd seen childhood as beneath him. A nuisance. An unfortunate period he was forced to endure on the road to becoming the adult he always knew he was inside.

The General had no children. He wanted no children. One of the policies he appreciated most about the army was that they didn't even allow children through the gate.

Nevertheless, the General had to admit it to himself—he was surprised. Despite his crackerjack military training and his experience fighting all manner of soldiers in every desert and jungle on the planet, he hadn't seen this one coming. He never would've predicted that the greatest threat to the United States of America would be a pair of squirts too young to be trusted to chop onions. Heck, the runt with the glasses barely looked strong enough to hold an onion, much less chop it with any sort of skill or efficiency.

The General had done it. He'd saved the nation and the world. He'd narrowed down the location of Gilded's base to somewhere within a single square mile northeast of the city. Then he had a stealth helicopter containing a squad of his mechanized infantry on standby, ready to take off at a moment's notice. When news stories started popping up about Gilded appearing in Nashville and Chicago and Denver, he thought for one terrifying minute that his target had sniffed him out and moved to a new location—maybe even a new city. The General had been so close, and yet it seemed his moment has passed him by again.

But the General wouldn't give up that easily. He'd worked too long and too hard. He ordered his surveillance teams to remain at their posts. He kept the helicopter fueled. And sure enough, last night Gilded returned.

Delta Team had been first to call it in: The target had been spotted in the air near Jimmy Carter Boulevard. Within two minutes, the General and his mechanized infantry were in the air as well.

The General had been coolly aware that the

mission might be the end for him. The adversary he was en route to intercept was more formidable than anything any general had ever faced before. But it was his duty, and if he were to die in the pursuit of it, then he'd die with honor.

Not one shot had been fired.

General Breckenridge shook his head at the pure irony of it. All the time and resources he'd spent designing his mechanized infantry to take down the deadliest of threats, and Gilded had somehow taken himself down. Radar showed him crashing in the thunderstorm, leaving the General and his mechanized infantry with little to do but land the helicopter and pick up the pieces. He hadn't even needed to call in the squads of additional mechanized units circling in the air overhead.

Which brought his thoughts back to the children.

As it turned out, the extraordinary technology that had bestowed tremendous abilities on Donald Plower was a golden cape. A cape that had allowed him to operate as Gilded for six long decades. But why had Plower placed such enormous destructive power in the hands of children? Allow children to play with matches and gasoline and they'll burn themselves. Allow them to play with an extraterrestrial weapon and they'll eventually burn everything. It was madness.

Madness, or was it part of a larger plan?

This wasn't the first time a child had been brought to the General's attention. The first, referred to as Subject One, he'd almost felt sorry for, a runaway scared and in hiding on the abandoned Plower farm.

Now there were three of them. The preliminary assessments didn't point to anything connecting Subject One to the two children he'd captured last night, but that didn't mean a connection wasn't there. Regardless, the General's subbasement was beginning to look less like a top-secret detention center and more like after-school day care.

The General supposed he needed to do something about the parents of his two new guests. People tended to notice when they'd misplaced their children, and they'd undoubtedly already begun calling neighbors, police, and anyone else who might help search for them. With Subject One, it hadn't been a problem because no one seemed to want her around. With the two boys, he sensed things weren't going to be as simple.

The door opened, and Corporal Slapped-Cheeks stepped into the office. "General," he puffed, short of breath, "I brought the doctor, like you ordered."

The General tightened his fingers in a white-knuckled clench.

"General . . . ?"

If only the corporal's mind were as well rounded

as his waistline. General Breckenridge darted his eyes at the open door.

Corporal Slapped-Cheeks looked around curiously, like he was waiting for something to dawn on him. Eventually, it did. "Oh!" His cheeks turned redder as he hurried from the room, pulling the door closed behind him.

The General's office was silent for a military cadence: hup, two, three, four.

knock knock

"Enter!" the General ordered gruffly.

The door opened again, and Corporal Slapped-Cheeks marched into the office. "General! I detained the doctor as ordered, sir!" He saluted, his posture ramrod straight.

"At ease, Corporal."

Corporal Slapped-Cheeks deflated. "She's waiting outside, General."

"Bring her in."

The corporal called cheerily over his shoulder, "You can come in now, Doctor!"

Dr. Petri entered with a file folder held in one hand.

"Dismissed, Corporal."

The corporal pivoted on his heels and exited the room.

The General reached into the top drawer of his

desk and took out a remote control. He pressed a button, and a panel slid back on the wall to reveal a large interactive TV screen behind it. He stood and touched the screen, and it came to life. It scrolled through data and reports concerning the two children who'd been brought in the night before: X-ray scans; magnetic imaging; blood and hair samples, DNA swabs, and fibers from their clothing. All taken while the prisoners were unconscious.

Dr. Petri was stunned. "My research. How did you . . . ?"

"Your research is my research. Everything that takes place in your lab is instantaneously synced with my system."

Dr. Petri frowned at the file folder, as if wondering why she'd bothered to bring it. "How long has that been the case?"

"Since the day you arrived." The General redirected Dr. Petri's attention to the screen. "Reviewing the medical profiles on each of the new subjects, it appears you've found no presence of contagion."

"Not yet. But this is only the preliminary examination. It's premature to interpret the data as conclusive. Remember, Subject One still exhibits no signs of contagion, but we can both agree she isn't . . . normal."

"Yes or no, Doctor. In your expert opinion—*limited* as it may be at this time—do Subjects Two and Three pose a public health hazard from having been in the presence of the Gilded technology for the past year?"

"No."

"Have they been escorted back to their sleeping quarters?"

"Yes. They need time to recover from the sedatives. I don't want to put any more stress on their systems than is necessary to confirm their general health."

The General returned to his chair. "Very well, Doctor. That will be all."

Instead of leaving, Dr. Petri stepped closer to the screen. "General, why are they all children? Subject One won't tell us how old she is, but based on skull size and length of the tibia and fibula, I estimate her to be between twelve and fifteen years old. These two boys seem about the same age." Dr. Petri scrutinized a scan of the runt. "This one could be a little younger," she corrected.

The General thumbed the remote, and the screen went dark. "That's not your concern, Doctor. Notify me if your laboratory tests reveal anything abnormal about them. Leave the rest to me. You're dismissed."

The General was perturbed to see that Dr. Petri wasn't leaving. No one ever remained in his presence after the General dismissed them. Oh, how he disliked her.

"Obedience to lawful authority is the foundation of manly character," the General said. Fine words to part company on. He always found General Robert E. Lee to be good for the soul.

"In case you haven't noticed, I'm not a man."

"That's no excuse."

Dr. Petri's jaw tightened. If the General wasn't careful, she was going to become a problem.

"General, what's going on here? What are you planning to do with these children?"

The General walked around his desk and opened the door. The corporal was standing just outside. He snapped to attention. "Sir!"

"Return the doctor to her lab, Corporal. Reprogram her access card. She's no longer permitted to leave the research level without my authorization."

"You can't do that!" Dr. Petri demanded.

"It's already done, Doctor. Enjoy your stay."

CHAPTER 13

MILES AWOKE SHIVERING ON A METAL COT. HE WAS feverish, cold and sweating at the same time, as if every cell in his body were alerting him that something was very wrong.

He didn't know where he was or how he'd gotten there. He didn't know why the concrete cell he was in was so small, or why there was a thick, plate-glass wall across the front. He didn't know why he was wearing a snug orange jumpsuit with what looked like ports for electrodes and devices he didn't want to imagine.

Most worrisome, Miles didn't know anything about what had happened between the arrival of the helicopter in the rainstorm and now. Hazy memories poked at the corners of his mind—the white room, the looming figures, the syringe. But if he tried to grasp the memories, they slipped away like water through his fingers.

Miles did know two things. He knew the cape

was missing. And he knew that was bad.

Miles pulled his knees up to his chest, holding himself tight. The cape was gone. The only thing in existence that could protect the world and he'd lost it—probably to the sort of bad guys who the world most needed protecting from. How many people were in trouble right now, looking to the sky for a glint of gold that wasn't going to come? If a disaster occurred while he was away . . . if one single person got hurt because Gilded wasn't there to help them . . .

A lump gathered in his throat, a dense tangle of emotion that, if he let it out, might never stop flowing.

His dad must be worried sick. Miles had just come back from a jaunt around the country and now he'd flown out into a thunderstorm and vanished. And Henry—

Oh my God. Henry.

He'd been with Miles when he was captured. If something had happened to Henry because of Miles, he'd never be able to live with the guilt.

Miles sat up on his cot. It took all his strength to speak the words, as though a dump truck were parked on his chest. "Henry? Are you here?"

There was a stretch of silence that seemed to last a year. Then a voice answered back, "Keep your voice down."

Miles scrambled to the front of the cell. He pressed his palms and cheek against the glass wall. He saw a hallway about ten feet wide with a row of cells running down each side, all of them appearing empty. "Henry!" he yelled. "Is that you? I'm over here!"

"I said, keep it down," the voice answered sternly. Miles had heard that tone many times lately. Usually accompanied by data recited from an unholstered smartphone.

Miles peered into the gloom of the cell across the corridor from his. Henry stepped out of the shadows. He, too, was clad in an orange jumpsuit. Rather than being snug, though, it hung a little loosely on his diminutive frame. Whoever had captured them, they apparently weren't expecting a prisoner who was sized extra-extra-small.

Henry gazed wide-eyed at Miles through the glass. He was scared. "They might be listening."

Miles was scared, too. "Any idea who . . . they are?"

"Military," Henry whispered cautiously, his eyes flitting about. "Army, I think. Judging by the stars on the leader's uniform, I'd say he was a general."

"A general . . ." It all started coming back to Miles. "I knew I recognized him. He was there in the parking garage the day I got the cape from the old man. And he was there again when I fought Calamity and the Unnd horde downtown." Miles looked around his cell. There was nothing except the cot and a metal chair. "Where are we?"

"I can't remember anything. They must've put us to sleep before they took us aboard the helicopter."

Miles's fingers touched the back of his neck. The site of the pinprick was still tender. "Why? What's the army got against us?"

"I think a better question is, how'd they find us? They caught up to you so fast after you crashed, it's like they were waiting for Gilded to show up. The only way that's possible is if they knew where you lived. But how could they?"

Miles hung his head. Just when he thought he couldn't feel any lousier, he'd found a way. "I . . . you know . . . might've cut a few corners."

Henry's eyes narrowed.

"I was going out on so many missions over the summer. I stopped switching up my travel routes to and from the apartment. For the past couple of months, I've been flying straight shots to emergencies and back."

Henry slid to the floor, his back slumped against the wall of his cell with his head hanging between his knees. "They cataloged your travel patterns and plotted them back to the part of the city they originated from. Like I warned you they would. Then all they had to do was stake out your area and wait for

Gilded to show himself. Textbook operation." Henry lifted his head. "Why couldn't you just listen to me?"

Miles had no answer.

"Can you bust us out of here?" a hushed voice asked.

If Miles's jumpsuit hadn't been snug, the sudden sound of an unknown, third voice would've made him leap right out of it.

Henry froze, feet planted and arms out, as if the floor had just shifted under his butt. "Who said that?"

"Me." It sounded like a girl's voice.

Henry scrambled to his feet. "Who's 'me'? Show yourself!"

"I'm over here."

Miles drew a bead on the direction the voice was coming from. It was the cell next to his. He pressed his cheek against the glass and strained his eyes, but it was no use; he couldn't get the angle. Whoever was there, they were completely blocked from his line of sight.

Not so for Henry. He was on the other side of the row, which gave him a clear look at the owner of the voice. Whatever he saw, it changed his demeanor immediately. "Hello, ma'am," he said genially, as if he were introducing himself to Mr. Harangue's new secretary. You'd never guess there were two tons of concrete block and two panes of thick glass separating him from the person he was talking to. "I'm Henry Matte. Who might you be?"

"Hurry. Bust us out." The voice sounded firmer. "Before they come back."

"Henry, who's over there?" Miles demanded.

"It's a girl."

"I can hear it's a girl. What's she look like?"

Henry considered the question. "Not pleased."

"I mean, is she a grown-up?" A dilemma like Miles and Henry were in, they could use some adult guidance.

"No," Henry answered, shaking his head.

"Then why'd you call her 'ma'am'?"

"She doesn't look like she's in the mood to be treated casually."

"You'll understand why, if you don't get us out of here. Please, kid," the voice begged. "I know you've never met me, but you have to trust me."

"It's Henry. My name is Henry. My associate's name is—"

"I heard you!" the voice snapped. "You're Henry. He's Miles. I'm Lenore. Okay? Is that a good enough introduction? This isn't summer camp. We've got to *go*."

Miles moved to the front corner of his cell, where he could be closest to Lenore. "We want to get out of here, too. Believe me. Do you have any idea where we are?"

"Some kind of soldier base, I think. I'm not even sure how long it's been."

"Why you?" Miles pressed.

"I didn't do anything wrong, if that's what you're asking. What does it matter, anyway? Just my luck. A couple of other inmates arrive, but one's the size of a roof rat and the other sounds about as sharp as a doorknob."

"Hey!" Henry protested.

Miles was having the mother of all bad days. He didn't appreciate the attitude. "Okay, Lenore. If you're so smart, why don't *you* get us out?"

"Isn't that your job?" Lenore sounded confused. "You know, I always imagined you'd be better at it."

"Better at what?" Miles huffed.

Miles heard Lenore's footsteps as she crept slowly to the front of her cell. If she was pressing herself into the corner like Miles was, only a few inches of concrete separated them. But it might as well have been the Great Wall of China.

"Help me," Lenore whispered. "If you're worried, I swear not to tell anyone I met Gilded."

Warnings blared in Miles's head. "Gilded?" he scoffed. "You think *I'm* Gilded? Like, the *superhero* Gilded? That's the craziest—"

"You and Henry were talking. I heard it. So stop pretending and get us out."

On the plus side, there was still only a handful out of the seven billion people in the world who knew Miles was the secret identity behind Gilded. On the negative side, in the last few hours, that handful had grown to include military kidnappers and an imprisoned girl.

Miles pointed at Henry accusingly. "You're the one who said it first."

"Oh, no, you don't," Henry answered. "You mentioned the old man and the cape."

"That could mean anything! You're the one who started talking about Gilded's home base!"

"You mean the home base you led them right to?"

"I said I was sorry about that!"

"Are you two always this whiny?" Lenore cut in. "Gilded never seemed whiny all the times I saw him on the news."

Lenore had a point. Now wasn't the time to be arguing with each other. And until Miles got the cape back, he didn't need a secret identity anyway.

"She's right, Henry. It doesn't matter. Let's just figure a way out of this place."

Henry nodded. "Agreed."

"What's to figure, Gilded? Punch a hole in the wall or something."

Hearing himself called by that name was like a rusty dagger being pushed into Miles's gut. Was he even still Gilded? "That's not how it works. It's hard to explain, but Gilded can't help us right now."

"Why are you acting like this?" Lenore said desperately. "Do you work for them? Did they put you in here to mess with my head?" Miles heard her slide down the glass wall of her cell. Her voice cracked. "Why can't everyone leave me alone?"

"Lenore?" Miles tried to sound comforting, despite not feeling very comforted himself. "My word hasn't been much good lately, but there are two things I can promise you. First, Henry and I aren't working for the people who brought us here. Second, we *will* get out."

Miles rapped his knuckles against the glass wall. It was solid all right. Still, it was only glass, maybe an inch thick at the most. It had to be breakable. He looked at Henry. "What do you think?"

Henry shrugged. "It's as good a place to start as any."

Miles grabbed the metal chair and dragged it over. Its legs scraped against the concrete floor like fingernails on a chalkboard.

"That won't work." Lenore groaned.

Miles imagined a big-league ballplayer at bat, winding back for a home run. He clenched his teeth and spun, swinging the chair at the glass with all the strength he could gather.

WHUNNNG!

The chair bounced off the glass, the impact sending shock waves like needles down Miles's arms. He dropped the chair, and it clattered to the ground.

"The glass is shatterproof." Lenore sounded deflated. "No matter how hard or how much you hit it, nothing happens. Believe me, I've tried."

Miles looked across at Henry. "Please tell me you have an idea."

Henry's shoulders sagged. "I don't. I really don't."

Suddenly, there was a hiss of air, followed by the sound of a door opening. Not a regular door, but something heavy and metal, like the door to a bank vault or a nuclear missile silo. Or a prison.

"They're coming!" Lenore whispered urgently.

Miles tried to look down the row of cells, as did Henry.

The heavy, hollow thud of hard-heeled boots approached. Miles searched for something—anything—to fight with. He grabbed the chair again.

"Who's there?" Henry called out.

The boot falls grew closer. What Miles wouldn't give to have the cape over his shoulders right now.

At last the threat revealed itself. If Miles hadn't been kidnapped via military helicopter, drugged, and imprisoned who-knows-where, he might've chuckled. He'd expected a jackbooted giant with a buzz cut and muscles until Sunday—basically the

Jammer, if he grew up and traded in his football jersey for camo. What he saw instead was a chubby, red-cheeked soldier who looked about as natural in his army fatigues as Miles would in a tutu.

No wonder the footsteps had sounded heavy. The man was less than six feet tall, but he looked like he hadn't been shy of two hundred fifty pounds since boot camp—and maybe not even then.

"Please refrain from hitting the glass," the soldier said. He was stern, like he'd caught Miles banging on the window of the gorilla exhibit at Zoo Atlanta. Miles recognized his voice as belonging to the pudgy man who'd found them in the rain. It was obvious the soldier's intent was to appear authoritative, but narrowing his eyes and pressing his lips together only caused his already small features to nearly get swallowed up by his jowls completely.

"Um . . . okay. Sorry about that," Miles said, setting the chair down gently. Crazy as it sounded, Miles didn't want to hurt the poor guy's feelings.

"Thanks for your prompt compliance," the soldier said. "I can tell we're going to get along just fine. My name is Corporal—"

"Corporal!" a booming voice cut in over an intercom.

The corporal snapped to attention. He saluted, but since there were no other military people present, he looked like he was saluting the air. "Sir!"

"No fraternizing with the prisoners. Have Subject Two brought to me for interrogation at once."

"Yes sir, sir!"

The corporal fumbled with a lanyard around his neck and produced a keycard from behind his fatigues. He swiped it through a scanner next to Miles's cell, and the glass wall slid upward silently.

"Step out and walk to the end of the hall," the corporal commanded. "And no funny stuff." The corporal punctuated that last bit by placing his hand on his holstered sidearm. He tried to look menacing, but all Miles could think was how bad he wanted to try some funny stuff—whatever that meant—just to see if the corporal's fat index finger could fit through the gun's trigger guard.

But what then? Miles didn't know where he was or what was waiting for him beyond the cells. Besides, Miles wasn't going anywhere without the cape. He had no idea how, but he was going to get it back. Until then, escape was out of the question.

Miles stepped out from the cell slowly, his arms in the air. The corporal seemed proud of that last bit, like he'd been searching his entire military career for someone to be intimidated by him and he'd finally found a thirteen-year-old who fit the bill.

The corporal pointed to the end of the hall. "March."

Henry pounded the heels of his fists on the front

of his cell. "Where are you taking him?" he demanded.

The corporal was firm. "You'll find out when it's your turn, Subject Three."

Miles stole a glance into Lenore's cell as he passed by. Her faced dropped when she saw him. She'd wanted a hero, and she'd gotten a kid. Miles was used to disappointing people, but usually it was people he already knew. Disappointing a total stranger who hadn't even had a chance to expect anything from him yet was a new low.

He wished he could help her. She looked so scared and vulnerable. She was—

"Keep moving!" the corporal ordered, prodding Miles in the back.

Miles headed down the row of cells, all of them empty except for Henry's and Lenore's. At the end waited an open vault door. At least he'd gotten that part right, though it did seem like an overabundance of security for a depowered superhero, a girl, and an undergrown gifted student.

"Good luck," Lenore called solemnly as Miles passed through the door. It was the last thing he heard before the corporal sealed the vault behind them.

CHAPTER 14

THE CORPORAL LED MILES THROUGH A WARREN OF drab, concrete corridors. They passed steel doors with keycard locks beside them, the only detail differentiating each of them being a room number etched into the front. No windows. Not a hint of sunlight or starry sky to indicate the time of day. With each echoing footstep, Miles's heart sank deeper into despair. The prison was sprawling and impossible for him to make sense of.

At last the corporal came to a door at the end of a hall. The number on the door read I-2. He swiped his keycard through the lock, and the door slid back with a pneumatic hiss.

The corporal pointed. "Inside."

Miles stepped into the room, and his blood turned to slushie.

Robots. A pair of them standing shoulder to shoulder, like some mechanical science-fiction soldiers from the future. They stood about seven feet tall, with tripod legs and two arms. Scratch that. The arms weren't exactly arms. Where their left forearms should be, there were wide barrels that looked like tank cannons stumped off and attached at the robots' elbows. In place of their right forearms there were weird tangles of saw blades and blowtorches and things Miles didn't even recognize. They reminded him of his dad's pocketknife, if the pocketknife went on a weight-lifting bender and spent six months in the gym. He'd never seen such terrifying examples of death machinery. And he'd witnessed the Unnd invasion firsthand, so that was saying something.

Miles flashed back to the night before. The smooth movement. The armored skin glinting in the rain. The viselike grip. These were the shadowy entities that had captured him.

The room was about the size of a tennis court. The robots were in the middle, like they were waiting for a ball they could bat back and forth. Or a person who could serve the same function.

The corporal prodded Miles forward until he was standing face to chest with the robots. Miles dared to gaze up at the cold, reflective visor that he assumed served as one of the robot's eyes. The robots were silent, switched off like toys on the shelf at the store, waiting to be taken home and played with. Miles imagined some high-ranking military official getting one for a present, turning it on, and then having his house demolished around him. Happy birthday, courtesy of the robo-soldiers from hell.

Miles swallowed hard on the lump forming in his throat as he pictured the long walk to get to this room and all the doors he passed along the way. If behind each of them waited machines like these . . . what chance did any kid have against that?

Apartment 2H. Chapman Middle. Josie. His dad.

Miles might not see any of them ever again.

"Admiring my mechanized infantry, I see."

The General stood in the doorway. His white hair and thick mustache were neatly trimmed. The breast of his olive-green uniform coat was adorned with more medals and ornaments than a Christmas tree. The creases of his slacks were sharp enough to slice a loaf of bread. He looked as though every aspect of his appearance has been paid the utmost attention.

"Sir!" the corporal shouted shrilly, saluting so fast Miles thought he might shave off the top of his own head. "Subject Two delivered as ordered, General, sir!"

The General's eye twitched almost imperceptibly. Miles reckoned that was as close as he ever came to flinching. "I can see that, Corporal. I'll notify you when I'm finished here."

The corporal spun on his heel and turned to leave,

walking smack into one of the robots. He bounced off it like a basketball hitting a brick wall.

The General clenched his jaw tight enough to pulverize a softer man's teeth to dust. "You're *dismissed*, Corporal."

The corporal hung his head and trudged off. He swiped his keycard through the lock again and exited the room, the door closing behind him with a soft, sad sigh.

The General clasped his hands behind his back and turned his focused attention to Miles. He didn't seem to be looking at Miles so much as looking through him, as though he already knew everything there was to know.

"At last," the General said smugly, "we meet."

"Who are you?" Miles tried not to sound as scared as he felt. "What do you want with me and my friend?"

"I will ask the questions here!" the General boomed. His voiced reverberated around the room. A silent moment passed, and then he tugged at the bottom of his coat, composing himself. "But perhaps you're correct. In the tradition of Ulysses S. Grant and Robert E. Lee convening at Appomattox Court House, we should grant each other the courtesy of talking as colleagues, not rivals. I am General Mortimer George Breckenridge, Unites States Army. And you are?"

The General was both terrifying and cordial at

the same time. Miles was too confused to speak.

The General bent at the waist, leaning forward to scrutinize Miles. "Refusal to answer isn't an option. Final warning. So let's try it again: I am General Mortimer George Breckenridge, Unites States Army. And you are?"

Miles wasn't sure how to respond. "Miles Taylor, Chapman Middle School?"

The General leaned in closer still. Another millimeter and the bristles of his mustache would tickle Miles's nose. "Where are you from?"

"Cedar Lake Apartments. You know where the Biscuit Barrel is on Jimmy Carter Boulevard? It's just down the street—"

"Enough!" The General snapped upright, his anger showing through again. Miles had never heard someone shout so loudly with their teeth clamped so tight. It was like mean-guy ventriloquism. "I should have expected you to show no respect for the etiquette of military discourse."

Miles wanted to point out that there wasn't a whole lot of etiquette in kidnapping people and holding them against their will, but he didn't want to set the General off any more than he already was.

"You may dispense with your insulting attempts at subterfuge. I've been following your exploits far longer than you realize. I know all about Donald

Plower and what was hidden beneath his onion farm. I know what happened in that parking garage last fall." The General thumped his index finger against his chest, setting his medals a-jangle. "I know everything." He declared it with such certitude, Miles almost believed him.

"I'm not trying to be disrespectful, Mr. Breckenridge—"

"*General* Breckenridge."

"General Breckenridge. Sorry."

The apology was sincere. If only he could make the General realize this was some kind of mix-up. Miles wasn't a villain. He was Gilded—the same Gilded who last year had fought alongside General Breckenridge himself against the Unnd. They were all on the same team.

"I don't understand what you want, General. We haven't done anything wrong or illegal, and I swear I don't know anyone named Donald Plower."

The General scoffed. "That's exactly what you wish me to believe. That you're an innocent little boy who wouldn't harm a kitten. But I won't be deceived by this . . . this . . ."—the General wagged a hand at Miles—"masquerade. I know better. It wasn't until after the alien invasion that I at last convinced the president that Gilded was the true threat. When he learns all that fearsome power was being wielded by a mere child? My God. Think of the disaster I've averted."

Miles exhaled heavily. What he was about to do was no small thing, but what choice was there? This was serious. The General needed to be convinced that Miles wasn't a bad guy. Fast. "If I tell the truth, will you promise not to tell the kid with the glasses I told you? Because I've disappointed him enough as it is."

"You have my oath as a military man," the General answered.

"Okay. I got the cape from an old man in a parking garage. See, he used to be Gilded, but he said he couldn't do it anymore. So he told me to take the cape and be the new Gilded. And that's what I've been doing. I'm the one who's been watching over Atlanta and, er"—Miles looked down at his feet—"a few farther-away places lately. It was me who helped stop the Unnd—those lizard-monster things who attacked the city were called the Unnd—from taking over Earth. You and your soldiers were getting beat, but I showed up and saved you. Remember?"

The General pressed his lips together.

Miles cleared his throat. "What I mean is, you're in the army. You want to protect people, just like I do. We can work together. You don't have to keep me here. Just give me back the cape and tell me what you need. As long as it's the right thing to do, I'll do it. You can trust me. I promise. I'm not a threat to anybody. I'm a hero."

"*YOU'RE NO HERO!*" The words blasted from the General's mouth.

"You have no right to speak that word," he continued. "You're a child. I'm fully aware of your cape and the power it grants you. Even if I hadn't discovered the truth long ago, I heard you and your friend discussing the matter in your cells."

A chill ran down Miles's spine. Henry was right—they were being spied on, watched like lab rats forced to play part in a cruel experiment.

The General seemed satisfied with himself. "Does that make you uncomfortable? It's how threats are dealt with in the real world. Throughout America's history, generals have stepped forward time and again to guide the nation through its darkest hours. Great men who've trained and prepared themselves to face the harshest dangers the world can offer. Would you have me believe that, because of you, all the danger is behind us? The notion is absurd. If not for me, you would have *become* our greatest danger. The cape is mine now. So are you, until I can be sure you'll never pose a threat to anyone ever again."

Miles almost couldn't ask the next question, for fear of what the answer might be. "How can I prove to you that we're on the same side?"

"You may not be able to," the General replied coolly. He didn't seem to care if Miles ever proved it to him or not.

"My dad." Miles's voice cracked. "Can I call him just to tell him where I am?"

The General shook his head. "He'll find out when the time is right. As will the parents of your accomplice. Everyone you've interacted with will be brought in for questioning. It's crucial that I learn who knows about the cape. Then I'll determine the steps necessary to contain this situation you've created."

"You won't!" Miles demanded. His dad, Henry, Henry's parents. They were all innocent. Miles couldn't bear to think that they were going to be interrogated or imprisoned because of him. And what about Josie? Was she also in the General's sights?

The General loomed closer. "I most certainly will. I'll wring every bit of information from all of you. I won't guarantee that it will be pleasant. But I guarantee you'll all tell me what I want to hear."

"No . . ." Miles backed away. "You're . . . you're insane."

"On the contrary. I'm a hero."

Miles couldn't breathe. He had to get away. Now.

He spun and nearly collided with one of the General's battle bots. He was paralyzed with fear. If he could just make it through the door, he'd stay on the loose until he found the cape. Once he had it, he'd break Henry out of his cell. Lenore, too. No one deserved to suffer at the hands of a madman like the General. Surely the cape would understand that. But first he had to get past the door.

Miles ran.

"Mechanized infantry!" the General bellowed. "Ten-*HUT!*"

The door was close. Miles was going to make it. He risked a glance over his shoulder and saw the robots' eye visors spark to life, glowing with sinister light like grocery checkout scanners of doom. The General stood motionless beside them.

"Ten-hutting, General Breckenridge," the battle bots replied in digitized unison.

Miles reached the door, his heart beating a thousand times a second. Safety was just on the other side. All he had to do was . . .

. . . locked. Miles has been so afraid of the General and his robo-soldiers, he'd completely forgotten about the keycard the corporal had used to unseal the door. No key, no way out.

"Detain Subject Two!" the General commanded. "Intact."

The machines rumbled to life in a chorus of spinning gears and firing pistons. "Detaining Subject Two, General Breckenridge."

Miles pressed his back against the door. The robots closed in. Large as they were, there was nothing lumbering about them. They moved fluidly and as a single unit, like mirror images of each other. It was coordinated precision at a level above the capacity of any human.

Miles frantically looked around the room. Surely the General had a keycard of his own hanging around his neck, right? He made a beeline for the General, pumping his legs as fast as he could.

A robot rolled in front of Miles, creating a barricade between him and the General. The tangle of tools on its right forearm shuffled, producing a large, three-fingered clamp.

Miles didn't have time to think. He hit the polished floor, sliding feet-first in his best impression of a big-league ballplayer stealing second base. His momentum carried him between the robot's legs just as its clamp snapped closed, pulling out some of his hairs.

Miles sprang to his feet and made his last dash for the General. Breckenridge held his pose, like he was engaging Miles in a game of chicken to see who'd flinch first.

Miles vowed to not let it be him. He spotted a lanyard around the General's neck and reached for it, his fingertips brushing the starched fabric of his collar.

Suddenly, there was a stabbing pain in Miles's left ankle. Before he knew what was happening, he was upside down and dangling, his hands reaching frantically for the lanyard.

A robot behind him had spun around to grab him with its clamp. Not exactly spun around, but rotated one hundred eighty degrees at the waist, so its top half faced Miles and its bottom half pointed the opposite way.

The robot hoisted Miles higher until he was staring directly into its visor. The clamp tightened on his ankle. Agony shot through Miles's leg like a jolt of electricity. His bones felt on the verge of shattering. He waited for the robot to blast him with its arm cannon or pull him to pieces with its assortment of beefed-up pocketknife tools. *Oh, God,* he thought, envisioning the top of his skull being peeled back. *Not the can opener. Anything but the can opener.*

"Stop!" Miles yelped. "I surrender!"

The robot's eye beam scanned Miles's face. "Subject Two detained, General Breckenridge. Intact."

The General watched Miles with interest. "You surrender?" the General pouted. "So easily? I expected more resistance."

Miles grimaced, his head swooning as his blood rushed into it. "Please. Don't kill me."

"Request granted." The General nodded at the

robot. "Mechanized infantry, release Subject Two."

"Releasing Subject Two, General Breckenridge." The robot opened its clamp, and Miles dropped to the floor. The robot spun its bottom half around to face the same direction as the top, while at the same time folding its clamp back into its assortment of tools. Then the robot stood stock-still, probably content to remain that way for all eternity, or until another kid required upending. Whichever came first.

The General leaned in, studying Miles with a sour frown. He was tipped forward so far, Miles didn't understand how he kept his balance. Maybe gravity followed the General's orders, too.

"My mechanized infantry is impressive, isn't it? I designed the units myself. Carefully selected each specification and weapon to create the perfect combat force for defeating large-scale threats. Threats like Gilded, you might say.

"Now here Gilded is"—the General clucked—"on the ground at my feet. But you aren't Gilded anymore. You're an insignificant boy. I very much wish I could've tested my special soldiers against the real Gilded, but alas, it wasn't to be."

Tears stung Miles's eyes. If only he could have one more chance with the cape. He'd be better this time. "If you want to see how your trash cans measure up," Miles dared, "give me the cape. We'll find out."

The General chuckled. "I think not, boy. A good leader never takes his victory for granted. But I admire your bravado." The General straightened. "Corporal!" he thundered.

The door at the end of the room flung open nearly before the General finished the word.

"Yes, sir, General Breckenridge, sir!" the corporal replied eagerly.

"Return Subject Two to his cell."

"Right away, General, sir!"

There was nothing Miles could do. He was defeated.

He limped out of the room with the corporal in tow.

CHAPTER 15

AS BEST MILES COULD FIGURE, THREE DAYS HAD passed.

Three days without breathing outside air or even so much as glancing through a window. Three days without being able to talk to his dad.

Was Mr. Taylor waiting at the police station for someone to tell him his son had been found? Was he hanging posters with Miles's yearbook photo on telephone poles and in store windows? Just thinking about how worried his dad must be made Miles feel even more dejected than he already was. Not an easy feat, given his current situation.

In the time since they'd arrived at General Breckenridge's Prison for the Completely Innocent, he and Henry had barely been able to talk. Miles had tried a few times, but Henry always shushed him. Miles didn't like it, but he understood why: They were being watched. They were only ever let out of their cells for meals and showers, always at the same times, and always accompanied by the corporal. As for the General, Miles hadn't seen him since they'd talked. It was like the General had forgotten about them.

Lenore had gone silent, too. Miles asked her questions about her family and where she was from and how she'd come to find herself jailed in a supermax military prison—you know, typical get-to-know-your-neighbor stuff—but Lenore never showed any interest in conversation. Maybe she was too afraid or too depressed, since Miles and Henry had turned out to be utterly useless as engineers of her escape. Or maybe, like Henry, she felt that saying nothing was better than being eavesdropped on.

If the solitary confinement wasn't unpleasant enough, the prison's amenities were downright nasty. Going to the bathroom was made possible by a small toilet and privacy screen that emerged as needed from a hidden compartment in the back of his cell. The sheets on his cot were as hard as month-old bread, and the food in the prison's cafeteria tasted like starched cotton.

It didn't take Miles long to figure out the prison's routine. He and Henry were woken each morning at oh-seven-hundred—which apparently was the army's long way of saying "seven a.m."—and escorted by the corporal to the cafeteria for breakfast, where their food was already on the table waiting for them. After breakfast came thirty minutes of cleanup time. They were permitted to shower, brush their teeth, and put on fresh jumpsuits identical to the ones they'd just taken off. All of this was conducted under the watchful eye of a pair of battle robots. Showering while armor-plated death dealers scanned them with their eye beams—nothing unsettling about that at all.

Lenore always went alone to cleanup time, finishing before Miles and Henry had their turn. That was the only time she ever left her cell. She hadn't joined them in the cafeteria once, but based on the reek wafting in the air whenever he returned from his meals, Miles figured she was given her food while they were gone. He'd tried asking her why she had all the extra security, but she refused to answer.

After everyone had been through cleanup time, they were allotted one hour of entertainment in their cells. "Entertainment" consisted of a hatch opening in the back wall, behind which was a plastic tub filled with books and toys. A short list of some of the items Miles had been asked to entertain himself with: a softback copy of *Curious George*, a half-dozen crayons and loose sheets of paper, two Wiffle balls, a wooden truck, and a twenty-four-piece puzzle of a cartoon dog running through a field of sunflowers.

The corporal tried to mix things up by rotating

the toys between Miles, Henry, and Lenore—sending Henry the wooden truck and giving Miles a sailboat instead—but it was all equally lame. Miles had seen better selections at his dentist's office.

Exactly sixty minutes after the entertainment period started—not one second more—the corporal's voice would screech over the loudspeaker for them to return the toys to the plastic tubs and the compartment in the wall would close again.

That was it. That was their life in captivity.

Miles and Henry were eating lunch on their third day. They sat across from each other at a bolted-down steel table in the cafeteria. Aside from a pair of battle robots standing guard at the cafeteria door—another thick door with a keycard lock—they were alone. Stark white and uninviting, the cafeteria didn't look all that much different from the lunchroom at Chapman Middle. On the one hand, Miles found the familiarity oddly comforting. On the other hand, he wondered why a school for law-abiding children had been designed to emulate a prison.

Miles looked glumly at his steel tray, sporking through his meal of liver and onions, onion hash, and onion rings. Every meal Miles and Henry were served was drowning in onions. At least they were given water to wash it down with, which Miles took to mean the kitchen hadn't devised a method for juicing onions yet. Thank God.

Henry shoveled a sporkful of chow into his mouth and choked it down. "Some say eating onions can help repel insects," he managed.

"No offense, Henry, but you keep eating onions, you're going to repel me."

"The odor is very mutual, I assure you."

Miles set down his spork and exhaled deeply. There was a weight that had been pressing down on his heart like a two-ton boulder since they'd arrived, and he couldn't carry it anymore.

"Henry, I screwed up."

"You think?" Henry groused.

"What I mean is, you tried to warn me and I wouldn't listen. I thought I didn't need anyone anymore. I got too big for my cape, and now . . ." Miles didn't want to go on, for fear that saying the next part out loud would make it come true. But it needed to be said. "And now I may have taken Gilded away from the world forever."

Henry said nothing.

"You're my best friend," Miles croaked. "Without you, I never would've been able to do the things I've done. You helped me figure out how the cape worked. You taught me how to be a superhero. So I promise: If we somehow get out of this place, we're going to be a team again. You and me. Because I was never Gilded all by myself. We were Gilded together."

Henry finally spoke. "You thought you had it all figured out, and now look where we are." He breathed out as though he was letting the bad feelings leave him. "But there's no point holding a grudge about it in here. As bad as this place is, it'd be a heck of a lot worse if you weren't in here with me. No matter where we are, we're still a team. Always will be." Henry extended his hand. "Apology accepted."

Miles shook Henry's hand. Never in his life had he been so relieved. "Thanks."

Henry scooped up a glob of onion hash and grimaced. "I should make you eat my next three days' meals as punishment."

"I don't know about you, but I don't plan to be here that long." Miles shot a surreptitious peek at the robots guards. "There has to be a way out of this place."

"There is," Henry affirmed, "and I'm going to find it." He stabbed his spork into an onion ring for emphasis.

There was a *beep* from the lock on the door, and Miles and Henry turned to see Lenore walk in with the corporal in front and a battle robot flanking her on either side. Actually, what she was doing couldn't really be classified as walking. It was more like shuffling because her ankles were locked in heavy manacles with a short chain between them. There was just enough length to keep her upright and moving forward, but that was it. Her wrists were bound, too, but there was no chain. The manacles were locked together, holding her arms in place.

The robots had each produced from their tool assortments a snare pole and a noose, like the one Miles had seen a woman from animal control use to catch a rabid raccoon. One of the loops was fastened around Lenore's neck and the other was around her waist. Miles couldn't imagine a tiger with a history of mauling circus-goers being treated with any more security.

It made no sense. Lenore was anything but threatening. She had slender arms and legs. Her head was bowed, her straight black hair hiding her face like a curtain. Her skin looked like the type that tanned rich brown, but it must've been forever since she'd experienced sunlight because it was nowhere near that shade. She looked miserable.

Miles and Henry exchanged an uneasy glance. They didn't say anything, but Miles could tell Henry was thinking the same thing he was: *At least we're not her.*

The robots led Lenore to a table on the other side of the cafeteria. They swapped out their snare poles for their three-fingered clamps and separated the manacles on Lenore's wrists, keeping a firm grasp on her arms as they sat her down. They attached each wrist manacle to a chain bolted down to the table, then set about doing the same to her ankles. Even scarier than the size and weight of the robots was the dexterity with which they moved. Their fingers were nimble enough to tie shoes on a pair of eggs.

"Subject One secure," the robots droned in unison. They backed away and stood against the wall behind Lenore.

The corporal pressed a button on the wall, and a mechanical dumbwaiter lowered from the ceiling, setting a tray of food and a single spork on the table in front of Lenore. "Behave yourself," the corporal warned, "or the General says next time you'll be punished for *two* weeks before you're allowed to eat outside of your cell." Then he turned and marched out of the room, the door closing behind him.

The room fell silent except for the rattling of Lenore's chains. She started on her onion hash and craned her neck down, so her spork could reach her mouth. There was just enough slack in the chains to allow her to feed herself, and not a single link more.

"Oh, man," Miles whispered. "They actually found a way to make eating onions worse."

Lenore shot Miles a menacing look he'd only ever seen on people twenty years older. She must have lived through a lot to have a stare like that in her repertoire. "Are you Italian?" she snapped.

"Um . . . I don't think so." The Taylor family had Scottish and Norwegian and a bunch of other -"ishes" and -"ians" in its gene pool. Miles had never really been able to keep them all straight. "Why?"

"Because you've got some roamin' eyes."

Miles blinked. "Huh?"

"It's a homophone," Henry said, grinning appreciatively. "She swapped out 'Roman' with 'roamin'.' She made a vocabulary joke."

"No wonder I didn't get it."

Henry picked up his tray and stood from the table. "I'm going to sit with her."

Before Miles could ask whether Henry was willing to risk death-by-can-opener, Henry was already crossing the room. The robots shifted their scanner eyes toward him, tracking his movement.

Henry set down his tray across from Lenore. "It's nice to be able to talk to you without glass walls separating us."

Lenore tensed, as though she might flick a sporkful of onion mush at him. Then her shoulders slumped. "Fine. Whatever. Just stay on your side of the table."

"Well, I'm very pleased to properly make your acquaintance." Henry held out his hand, offering to shake.

Lenore frowned, rattling the chains binding her to the table. "A little tied up here."

Henry adjusted his glasses. "Right. Sorry about that." He leaned forward, bringing his hand toward hers.

Lenore jerked her hands back, pulling the chains taut. "I said stay on your side!"

Miles eyed the battle robots uneasily. "Guys? Maybe we should keep it down."

Henry withdrew his hand, looking confused. Miles didn't understand what the big deal was either. Lenore was acting like Henry had hurt her, when all he'd wanted to do was be polite.

Lenore sat forward slowly, like she was carefully considering her every move. "If you're going to sit, sit. Just don't even think about touching me."

"Fair enough." Henry nodded, taking his seat. Then he waved Miles over. "Come eat with us."

Miles kept his eyes on the robots as he walked over and sat beside Henry. "Are you sure we should be talking so much?"

Henry shrugged. "It's just a little harmless introduction. So, Lenore," he began, "where are you from?" He asked the question casually, as though Lenore was a new student at Chapman and Mr. Harangue had asked him to show her around campus.

"Toombs County. A town called Vidalia."

"Like the onion?" The question had leaped to the front of Miles's mind.

Lenore swallowed down a mouthful of onion ring. "That's right. What of it?"

"Oh, nothing," Miles answered. "Just kind of ironic, don't you think? Our current diet being what it is."

"Not ironic. Irony involves opposites." Lenore pushed her onion hash around her tray. "This is more like an unhappy coincidence."

Henry smiled goofily. Never mind Lenore's standoffishness and generally peculiar demeanor. She'd displayed proficiency in two separate literary devices in the span of five minutes. "You really know your language arts."

Oh, brother. As far as pickup lines went, it sounded more like a put-down.

Miles cut in. "What can you tell us about this place? Where are we?"

Lenore shrugged. "Somewhere in Georgia, I think. They brought me here chained in the back of a freight truck. The sun was hitting the left side of the truck before sundown, so that means we went north. The drive wasn't much more than three hours from the farm where they grabbed me up."

"How long ago was that?"

"I don't know exactly," Lenore answered. "A few months?"

"A few *months*?" The words stabbed Miles like a spike through his heart. Was the General planning to keep him locked up for months? Years?

"Maybe longer. Do you . . . ?" Lenore paused, like she was mustering the courage to ask her question. "Do you know what month it is?"

"August," Henry answered carefully.

Lenore lowered her eyes. "Then I'm fourteen now. Happy birthday to me." She dropped her spork onto her tray and nudged it away.

Henry glanced at Lenore's chains. "If you don't mind me asking," he pressed, "why you? Miles and I know why they brought us here. What did you do?"

Lenore studied Miles, then Henry, then Miles again. "Nothing. One day, out of the blue, there was a bunch of stuff going on at the old Plower onion farm back home in Vidalia. General Breckenridge and his troops dug something up out of the ground. I only ever saw it draped under canvas, but I could tell it was big. Once they had it, I figured they'd move on. But they caught me watching them and arrested me. They told me I was a danger to other people, like I might make people sick or something. I've been here ever since."

An onion farm . . . Plower . . .

"Plower!" Miles blurted.

Lenore fishhooked an eyebrow. "You been there?"

"No. But the General said something about a guy named Donald Plower. He mentioned the parking garage where I met Gilded, too. Did you know Donald Plower?"

Lenore shrugged, clinking her chains against the table. "No one did. He was more a local legend. Like a ghost story. The onion farm had been in his family for generations, but one day he just up and left. No explanation. No good-byes. Some said he moved to Atlanta, but no one in Vidalia ever heard from him again. That all happened a long time before I was born, but people still talk about it around town. The farm was abandoned for decades. Right up until the General and his troops arrived."

"Curious," Henry said distantly. If Miles had X-ray vision, he was certain he would've seen gears turning in Henry's brain. He'd been given a clue, and he was going to suss it out.

Henry changed tacks. "What about your parents? They must be looking for you, right?"

"We aren't close." Lenore stated it like a fact. This wasn't the typical kid-says-their-parents-don't-care-what-happens-to-them-but-they-know-their-parents-really-do-care-what-happens-to-them talk. This was no-joke-my-parents-really-don't-care-what-happens-to-me talk. It was the loneliest thing Miles had ever heard.

"They're still your parents," Miles said. "They'll be looking for you." He thought again of his dad. Miles's last words to him had been spoken in anger. What if those were the final words they ever shared between them? The thought hit Miles like one of the Jammer's punches to the gut.

Lenore's jaw clenched. "No."

"What do you mean? They—"

"Just drop it!" Lenore shouted. She squeezed her fists, like she was trying to keep something from exploding within.

The moment passed, and Lenore deflated. She dabbed her eyes with the back of her wrist. Realizing Miles was watching, she flicked her tray of food, sending it skidding down the table. She may have been small for fourteen, but there was no doubting she was strong. "I don't know what makes me tear up worse," she grumbled. "The onions, or all these dumb questions."

Henry leaned forward, gesturing for Miles and Lenore to do the same. "One thing is clear," he whispered. "If we're going to get out of here, we have to do it ourselves. This is a top-secret military base. Our friends and parents can search for us all they want, but they won't be able to find us." He leaned in even closer. "Lenore, tell me everything you know about this place."

Lenore motioned at their surroundings. Hands chained down the way they were, the movement was stifled, like a bird trying to stretch stunted wings. "What's there to tell? You've been here only three days, but what you see is what you get. Nothing ever changes."

"Why don't they just feed us in our cells?" Henry whispered, shooting a glance at Lenore's chains. "It'd be a lot easier than all the added security measures."

Lenore frowned. "I think they go through our cells while we're gone. Sometimes I'll go back and my pillow won't be the way I left it. Or the sheets will have been changed, but still messed up, like they don't want me to know they changed them. Maybe that's how they do housekeeping. Or maybe they want to check we're not hiding anything that we could use to try to escape. Or it could just be another way of monitoring us." She looked down at a sensor pad stitched into her jumpsuit over her heart. "Like these outfits they make us wear. All full of wires and sensors, so they can study us."

"What are all the chains about?" Miles asked. "Did you do something bad?"

"Yeah." Lenore ran her fingers over the surface of the table, which Miles noticed was pretty beat-up, as though someone had taken a ball-peen hammer to it. "I acted up. That's why I wasn't allowed in the cafeteria the past week."

Henry adjusted his glasses, looking at the dents warily. "Can you think of anything else? Something out of the ordinary that we can use. Even if it's really small."

Lenore shook her head. "The only thing that's happened out of the ordinary was you two arriving. That sure threw them into a fit. Jerry said they had to come up with all new procedures for dealing with you."

"Jerry?" Miles asked. "Who's Jerry? You mean General Breckenridge?"

"The corporal who lets us in and out of the cells. He's the only other person I've talked to since they dumped me here. I know there are more soldiers because I spotted some from the back of the truck the day I arrived, but they must all be aboveground or something. Here in the prison complex, it's just Jerry and them." Lenore nodded at the robots posted behind her. Their red eye scanners pulsed rhythmically, like lights on computers in power-save mode. It was eerie how easy they were to forget about. Large and menacing as they were, they faded into the background when they weren't active.

"Anyway, you two showing up really got Jerry flustered. His cheeks were so red, I thought they'd catch fire. He said the routine was disrupted, and the General hates when his routine gets disrupted. He's all about such-and-such time *on the dot*, and such-and-such allotment of food *to the ounce*, and on and on. I think that's why he made the robots—so they could follow the routine to the littlest detail. Plus, you know, to kill stuff."

"You're sure there isn't more?" Henry pressed. "You never do anything else?"

Lenore's face went ashen. Her fingers moved to a port sewn into the notch of her elbow. "No. Nothing else."

"Lenore, it's important that you tell me everything."

Lenore looked like she might vomit—and not just because she had a bellyful of onions. "There's . . . I'm not sure. Once a week, they take me to a lab. I don't remember much after. I wake up back in my cell, but . . ." Her face tightened, straining for a memory just beyond her grasp. "I can tell they did something to me. I just can't remember what."

Now Miles felt nauseous. He thought of the white room and the balloon suits. The warm sensation clouding his brain and then darkness. "You must remember something," he urged. "Think."

"I don't . . ." For a second Lenore looked terrified. Then she shook her head. "I can't remember. Stop asking me about it."

The three of them fell into an uncomfortable silence.

As if on cue, the two robots that had escorted

Lenore whirred to life. "Thirteen hundred hours," they announced in unison. "Midday meal has ended. Subjects One, Two, and Three are required to return to their cells."

The robots rolled forward, their three-fingered clamps unchaining Lenore's wrists and ankles and connecting them together again. They stood her up, once again producing snare poles from their tool assortments and looping them around her neck and waist. Miles and Henry were powerless to do anything but watch.

Lenore showed Henry a grim smile, like she was somehow at peace with the inevitability of it all. "Thanks for eating with me."

"It was our pleasure," Henry said.

Lenore looked sheepishly at Miles. "Look . . . I'm sorry I got angry when you asked about my parents. I'm not used to talking much, is all." She held forward one hand, offering Miles a fist bump. It was a small gesture, made even smaller by her limited ability to do much more than stand and breathe. She looked humiliated and sad and scared all at once. "No hard feelings?"

"No hard feelings," Miles agreed. He brought his own fist forward, leaning in to bump Lenore's in return.

Suddenly, Miles lost his balance. Before he knew

what had happened, he was sprawled facedown on the cold tile.

"You all right, Miles?" Henry asked, his eyes wide with dismay.

Miles rolled over, massaging his cheek where it had face-planted the floor. "Yeah. Guess I slipped."

Lenore looked down at Miles, her hands bound in front of her. Miles could swear he spotted the hint of a smirk beneath her resigned expression. "Watch yourself."

The robots tugged on their loops, jerking Lenore forward. She turned her back and shuffled out of the room.

CHAPTER 16

GENERAL BRECKENRIDGE HAD TRIED EVERY battlefield weapon known to man—and some that were still top secret—to test the cape's limits.

Machine guns. Flamethrowers. Grenade launchers. He'd stacked a pyramid of mines and detonated them while he was crouched behind a wall of sandbags. The blast had rattled the fillings in his molars.

So much firepower . . . with no effect. Not a mark or tear.

The cape was indestructible.

The General stood in his bunker, a vast concrete room far below Dobbins Air Reserve Base. Accessible only by elevator, it was in this same bunker that the General had tested the first generation of his mechanized infantry, gone back to the design board, and tested them again. He'd had the bunker built specifically for that purpose, so no outsiders would know he was crafting the army of the future. Now the bunker was hiding something far more powerful—the secret of Gilded himself.

The bunker was empty, save for the General. The golden cape was fastened by clamps to the chipped, cracked concrete wall. He couldn't explain what it was manufactured from or how it was able to give off a golden glow, despite the lack of any detectable power source. Part of the problem was that there wasn't a way to sample the darn thing. All attempts to remove even a single thread had resulted in broken tools. He'd considered consulting Dr. Petri, but he preferred that she continue her laboratory tests on Subject Two and his runt friend (he barely qualified for being called Subject Three—more like Subject Two-and-a-Half). Besides, the General wasn't sure how much he could trust her with something so invaluable.

The General stepped closer to the cape, his combat boots sending used bullet casings clattering across the floor. He'd spent the past half hour firing at it with a chain gun at a rate of five hundred rounds per minute. Each time a bullet bounced off the fabric, it was like witnessing another tiny miracle.

He removed the cape from the clamps. It's flawless fabric slid silkily through his hands, a soft hum warming his fingertips. It was as thin and as light as a pillowcase, making its unearthly resilience even more fascinating. If only the cape's inner workings weren't shrouded in so much mystery.

The General's best guess was that using the cape required connecting its rudimentary clasp mechanism. He'd decided not to test the theory until the cape had been studied further. What if, once it was worn, it emitted lethal radiation? What if it caused an explosion? The dangers could be significant.

On the other hand . . .

The General *was* in a fortified concrete bunker designed to withstand detonations. Any danger the cape might pose could certainly be contained within.

The cape glowed. It hummed. It was calling to him. He couldn't wait any longer.

He turned to a Humvee, appraising his reflection in the window. He was aged and hardened, nearing the end of his life's journey.

No. The real journey was about to begin.

The General draped the cape over his shoulders. He took a long, lingering gaze at his reflection.

He was magnificent.

He wasn't a child playing dress up. He was a serious commander intent on serious business.

The first time he'd seen the cape up close was

the day the aliens attacked. What had the boy called them? The Unnd. They'd torn through the General's troops with hardly any effort at all. Then Gilded had arrived, and the tide of the battle turned. Afterward, it was as though the General had never even been there, had never found the city in a desperate moment and thrown himself in harm's way. Everyone waved at Gilded, exclaiming he was their hero.

A child. It was laughable.

Now it was the General's turn. When citizens jubilantly looked skyward, it would be him they saw. When they put their heads on their pillows, it would be thoughts of him that would grant them peaceful dreams. With the cape, he would be the champion of every desperate moment that arose. He vowed it.

The clasp halves moved in his fingers.

Just the smallest twitch, but it was there—the halves were pulling themselves together. Surely they sensed the General was worthy. The man the cape had been waiting for. The man the cape deserved. The General would do his duty, protecting America against all enemies terrestrial and alien.

The clasp halves jumped from his hands and clicked together.

Lock and load.

CAN...
CAN IT BE?

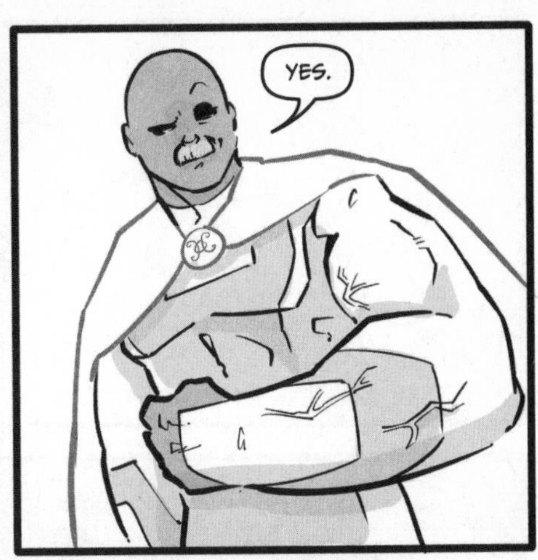
YES.

YES.
YES!

THE STRENGTH! THE POWER!
KRAKOOOM

AT LAST.

NO ONE WILL DARE OPPOSE ME NOW!
BOOKS WILL BE WRITTEN ABOUT ME! I'LL BE THE GREATEST MILITARY COMMANDER THE WORLD HAS EVER SEEN!

CLICK

The General staggered. The sensations of strength and vigor evaporated as quickly as they'd overcome him. He was woozy, his head reeling like the blood had been let out of it.

"No!" he bellowed. Acrid smoke from the tires of the burning Humvee seared his lungs. He stumbled to the wall, leaning on it for support.

He didn't understand. Why had the cape been operational for only a few moments—a few glorious, exhilarating moments? He'd witnessed the cape work for far longer spans of time. His surveillance teams had recorded hours of footage proving it.

The General saw the clasp halves dangling lifelessly over his shoulders. Of course. How simple. The mechanism had accidentally come undone when the General—Gilded—had hurled the Humvee. No cause for alarm. Just put the clasp halves back together—

They fell apart again.

And again.

And again and again and again.

The clasp wouldn't stay joined. The General noticed the cape was no longer glowing. No soft hum. Something was wrong, and he knew not what.

But the boy would know. He'd spent a year with the cape. As much as General Breckenridge despised admitting it, a mere child understood this immaculate golden instrument of warfare better than he did.

The General pressed an intercom on the wall. "Corporal!" he shouted.

"Yes, sir, General, sir!" the speaker squelched in reply.

"There's been an incident with one of the Humvees. Have the air in the bunker vented. Then have Subject Two sedated and brought to me."

CHAPTER 17

IT WAS LUNCHTIME IN THE CAFETERIA AGAIN.

Miles had eaten as much of his French onion soup as he could stomach, which was pretty much limited to the baked cheese at the top of the bowl and the soggy lump of bread floating just beneath it. For reasons that made no sense to Miles, Lenore preferred to get tangled in her chains during her meals—bringing the food to her mouth slowly, chewing painstakingly—rather than let anyone help her eat. He couldn't fathom what could cause a kid to become so closed off.

They all sat in silence. Miles pushed away his tray and glanced at the robots guarding the door. They looked idle. He leaned closer to Henry, turning his head so as not to knock him out with onion breath. "Any ideas yet on how to break out of here?" he whispered.

A few minutes earlier, Henry had started watching the wall clock intently. Miles had noticed that he'd been doing that more lately, keeping one eye on the time while they moved from their cells to the cafeteria or the showers and back again. He was starting to worry his best friend was losing his grip.

"Henry?"

"I'm working on it," Henry answered without taking his eyes off the clock. "Just keep talking with Lenore."

"I can't think of anything else to ask her," Miles pressed. "Let me help."

Henry darted his eyes at Miles. "Talking to Lenore *is* helping. It'll keep the attention off me."

"Got it." Miles turned to Lenore. "So, Lenore," he said loudly. "What's it like living in Vidalia?"

Lenore rolled her eyes. "Is that a serious question? Are we pretending we aren't locked up now?"

Miles shrugged. "We're here. We have to talk about something."

Miles couldn't help being curious. Maybe it was because everything about Lenore was shrouded in mystery. Maybe it just helped him keep his mind off the fact that he might never see daylight again. Either way, she was something to dwell on.

"No, we don't."

"Come on," Miles prodded. "What's the big secret? You go first. Then I'll tell you anything you want to know about me."

Lenore tossed her spork onto the table, her chains *clink-clinking*. "Okay, fine. What's life like in Vidalia? I don't have any parents, that's what life is like. They gave me up for adoption when I was one. I've been in and out of a million foster homes my whole life. The nice ones don't want me around longer than I have to be. The bad ones I run away from. I split from the last one about a month before the General found me. That's why I was hiding on the abandoned farm. Happy now?" Lenore recited it all matter-of-factly, like she was running down a book report.

"Oh God," Miles said. "I didn't know. I'm sorry."

"See, that's why I don't like to talk about it. As soon as people hear, they treat me different. Apologize and act like I'm some stray dog. Maybe I like being on my own. You ever think about that? No one pretending they want to take care of me so they can cash a check from the government. No so-called friends making fun of me behind my back."

"Do you . . . ? I mean, did anyone ever . . . ?"

"Tell me why my parents gave me up?" Lenore raised her wrists, showing Miles the manacles clamped over them. "It's obvious, doorknob. They gave me up because there's something wrong with me."

If he thought she'd let him, Miles would've hugged her. He knew the feeling of being kicked to the curb by the people who were supposed to love you most.

"My mom . . . she left, too. Went to Florida with some guy named Jack."

Lenore scoffed. "That supposed to make us the same? Well, we're not. You've got a home and a dad who's worried about you. In the past year, the only place I've slept more than a month straight is this prison. You don't know the first thing about what it's like to be me."

She was right. Miles *couldn't* relate, and he was lucky because of it. He missed his dad even more. "I'm sorry," he repeated.

"Next time I say I don't want to talk about something, take the hint."

Miles looked to Henry for a bailout, but he was still focused on the clock.

The time was 12:59. The second hand spun toward the vertical position.

"Fifty-six, fifty-seven, fifty-eight," Henry mumbled. "One o'clock." He whipped his head around to watch the cafeteria door.

At that moment, the door opened. Jerry entered, and the two robots on guard duty whirred to life.

"Thirteen hundred hours!" Jerry announced. "Midday meal has ended."

"Routine," Henry said.

Miles and Henry stood, and Lenore's pair of dedicated robot wardens rolled forward to unchain her from the table. She started to get up, but the shackle around her right ankle caught on the leg of the table, and she teetered over. Wrists and ankles bound, she couldn't do anything to break her fall. Her head was on a collision course with the cold, hard floor.

Everything happened too fast for Miles to see. Henry rushed forward to help, and then there was a dull, heavy *BOING!*, like the sound of a water balloon rebounding off a trampoline. Henry sailed backward, crashing into Miles and knocking them both to the ground. Henry's glasses skittered across the tile.

Miles shook off the impact and staggered to his feet. "What'd you do that for?" he yelled angrily at the robots. "Henry was just trying to keep her from falling!"

The robots flashed their eye beams across Miles's face. They'd already dropped their loops over Lenore to immobilize her. Her focus was on Henry, though. She looked at him guiltily.

Jerry stepped between Miles and the robots. "Don't confront the mechanized infantry," he warned. "You'll get hurt."

"You don't care about us!" Miles snapped. "You just follow the General's orders! You're no better than these stupid machines!"

Jerry's cheeks flushed red as though Miles had smacked him. "That wasn't very nice," he grumbled.

"I'm fine, Miles." Henry was on his feet and sliding his glasses back onto his face. "Don't make things worse for us."

"How could things get any worse? We're *hostages*!" Miles was drained. If he didn't pull himself together, he might cry.

"Miles," Henry stated, glancing surreptitiously at Lenore. "It's going to be okay."

"It's not," Miles croaked.

Henry's hand shot up to grab Miles's upper arm, squeezing it like a vise. He looked dead straight into Miles's eyes. "It's going to be okay," he repeated.

Miles's shoulders sagged in defeat. "Okay, Henry. Okay. Let's just go back to our cells."

Jerry raised a hand, holding Miles back. "Not you. The General wants to see you in the lab."

Miles's hair stood on end. He took a step back. "No. I'm going back to my cell."

"Orders are orders," Jerry said sternly. He reached for Miles again.

Miles smacked Jerry's hand away. "I don't care about your stupid orders!" he shouted.

Jerry massaged his hand and turned to one of the robots. "Escort Subject Two to the lab."

The robot shuffled through its attachments and produced something that looked like a Taser. The end crackled with electricity. "Escorting Subject Two."

Miles's heart quickened. "Don't come near me!"

"What's this about?" Henry protested. "Where are you taking him?"

The robot brought the Taser closer. Miles knew he should obey, but he couldn't gather the guts to put one foot in front of the other. He didn't want to see the General. He didn't want to go to the lab.

zzzt

A jolt ripped through Miles's body. There was a sick, metallic taste in his mouth. Over his buzzing ears, he heard Henry screaming.

"Leave him alone!"

A clamp gripped Miles's neck, the pain cutting through the daze. Another robot closed in on Henry. Miles's mistakes had gotten Henry into enough trouble. He wasn't going to let him get hurt, too.

"Stop!" Miles shouted.

The robot paused.

"Just don't hurt them." Miles's tongue was heavy. "I won't fight. Take me away."

The pinch of a needle plunged into Miles's neck.

He was unconscious before he hit the floor.

CHAPTER 18

MILES'S HEAD FELT LIKE IT WAS PACKED WITH blow-dried cotton balls—fluffy and airy and tangled all at the same time. He started to come around, his vision slowly clearing as the fog lifted from his brain. He squinted against the harsh light reflecting off white walls, and terror racked him.

He was in a lab.

His adrenaline spiked, flushing what was left of the knockout drug from his brain. He bolted upright on the steel table.

There was the soft whishing sound of a door sliding open, and frigid air blasted into the room. The General appeared beside him. "Welcome, Subject Two," he said genially. "I apologize for not seeing you the past few days. I've been focusing on other matters. However, it's time we had a serious talk."

The General seemed different from last time. More polite. Nice even.

"First tell me why you keep drugging me." Miles tried to sound confident, but he knew his voice was shaky. "Then we can talk."

"I apologize. My mechanized infantry can sometimes be overzealous in the execution of my orders. As for my own behavior"—the General clasped his hands behind his back—"I worry that it caused us to start off poorly. I blame the rigors of my job. It can sometimes put me in a sour mood."

Miles wasn't sure how to respond. In a weird way, the General's politeness was scarier than his anger. "Apology accepted?"

"Splendid!" The General clapped his hands together and stepped toward Miles excitedly. "I've thought a lot about what you said to me the first time we spoke. Perhaps we do have a similar goal—we both want what's best for this nation. You do want that, don't you, Miles? Do you mind if I call you Miles?"

"No. I mean, yes," Miles stammered. "I mean, no, I don't mind if you call me 'Miles.' Yes, I do want what's best."

"A man of sincerity. How admirable. Since we both want what's best, Miles . . . tell me how to use the cape."

Miles leaned away, a mental alarm sounding in his head. "I've got a better idea. Since we both want the same thing, why don't you give me back the cape and we'll forget any of this ever happened."

The General shook his head. "You don't honestly believe yourself qualified to be Gilded, do you? You've made a decent show of it, true, but you're only a child. A decent show isn't good enough. Not with the future of the United States at stake. The person who wears the cape should have discipline. Training. A command of the arts of national defense and warfare. Do you have any of those things?"

Miles understood where the conversation was headed, and he didn't like it one bit. Maybe there was truth to what the General said. Maybe Miles wasn't good enough to wear the cape anymore. Maybe he never had been. But he knew for sure that the General wasn't good enough, either. "Sure don't. But I know how the cape works, which is more than I can say for you."

The corner of the General's mustache twitched. "Is that so?"

"Yeah, that's so." Miles crossed his arms. "I'm not going to tell you anything."

The General's demeanor changed instantly. "Yes," he hissed through clenched teeth, "you will. Mechanized infantry, restrain Subject Two."

A pair of battle robots rolled into the room. "Restraining, General Breckenridge."

Before Miles could try to get away, the robots

gripped him in their clamps. They pressed him down so forcefully, he thought the table might break beneath him. "Let me go!" he yelled.

"No, I don't think I will." The General reached into his pocket and took out a syringe filled with a sickly yellow liquid. "But I'll help you get more comfortable."

The syringe plunged into Miles's arm, entering through a port sewn into his jumpsuit. A sharp pain shot up to his shoulder. The General jerked the syringe back out, the last drops of liquid spurting from the needle.

Miles flopped and squirmed, trying to break free. "What was that? Tell me what you stuck me with!"

"A little something to make you more compliant." The General smiled as though he'd just done Miles a favor. He hadn't. "I have a few questions, and it's imperative that you're truthful."

Miles felt euphoric, like floating on a lazy river in the summer sun. His mind was split in two. One side knew there was a mystery concoction spreading throughout his bloodstream. The other side didn't care. ". . . I can be truthful. . . . I don't like you, General. . . ."

"Good," the General cooed. "That's very good. Now let's talk about the golden cape. Let's talk about Gilded."

The mention of the cape made Miles feel warm,

like a pleasant memory was coming back to him. "I like the cape. . . ."

"I do as well, Miles. It's very nice. Tell me how it works. How does it make you Gilded?"

". . . Good . . . good . . ."

The General's face tightened. "Yes!" he snapped. "The cape is good! Now tell me!"

Miles tried to focus, to assert his will over the part of him that wouldn't shut up. He couldn't. Whatever was in that syringe, it made it impossible for him to not speak the truth. "I was bad. . . . I used to be good. . . . You're bad . . ."

"Enough!" The General slammed his fist on the table. He reached into his pocket and took out a second syringe. He bit the cap off and spat it away, clutching the syringe in his fist like a combat knife, ready to drive it into Miles.

There was a whishing sound a thousand miles away. Cool air tickled Miles's face like butterflies.

"What's going on here?" a voice demanded.

Miles craned his neck to see a woman in a white lab coat standing behind him. Her black hair was pulled back in a ponytail, revealing sharp, intelligent eyes.

"I'm conducting an interrogation, Dr. Petri," the General said gruffly. "Your services are not required."

"An interrogation?" The doctor raced to Miles's

side, shining a pen flashlight into his pupil.

"Bright . . ."

The doctor was furious. "What did you give him?" She opened the drawer beneath the table. "This wasn't our agreement, General. I'm responsible for the health and safety of these children."

"And *I* am responsible for the safety of the nation! Subject Two is hiding information of vital national interest!"

Dr. Petri scowled. "You'll have to find another way of getting it out of him." She placed a gentle hand on Miles's shoulder. "This is going to pinch."

". . . I don't like shots. . . ."

Another syringe stabbed Miles's arm. The euphoric feeling receded, the two separate parts of him merging into a single person again.

The General snatched the doctor's wrist and spun her around. "This is insubordination!" He shoved her away, raising his syringe over Miles.

"I wouldn't do that, General." The doctor massaged her wrist, grimacing. "A second dose could kill him. If he's as important as you say, I'm betting you don't want to risk that."

"Gah!" The General threw the syringe against the wall, shattering it. "For how long?"

"Twenty-four hours. Forty-eight to be safe." She pushed past the General and leaned over Miles again.

"I'm sorry. This shouldn't have happened," she said quietly.

Miles was about to thank her. But with the General's truth mix counteracted, he was able to focus. He'd heard her voice before, and the memory of it filled him with terror. "You were there that first day! In the balloon suit! Get away from me!"

The doctor pulled back. "It's not what you think—"

Miles couldn't help it. He started to cry. All the fear and guilt and failure flooded out of him. He couldn't hold it in a single second longer. "I want to go home!"

The General stomped forward. "Home? You are *never* going home. This is only the beginning. I'm going to learn everything about the cape, and you *will* teach me."

If Miles could go back in time, he'd do everything differently. He'd listen to Henry and his dad. He'd notice the warning signs when he started to go astray. He wouldn't help people because he wanted to be Gilded; he'd be Gilded because he wanted to help people.

Henry was right. Miles had started thinking of people's tragedies and miseries as an excuse to feel better about himself. What did that say about him? Who had he become? He hadn't become a superhero, that was certain. He'd become a selfish, self-involved jerk. He wasn't any different from the General. He might not have kidnapped or interrogated anyone, but what he'd done was just as wrong. And now there was no fixing it.

"Please," Miles sobbed. "No more."

The General seethed. "Oh, there'll be more. There'll be *plenty* more. And if you won't talk, then I'll persuade your runt friend. Or your father, or anyone else you care about."

"General!" Dr. Petri shouted. "That's enough! If you don't leave the lab this instant, I'm going to report your actions to your superiors. You may be a general, but you aren't God."

The General stiffened. "No, doctor. It's *you* who's leaving. Your security clearance is revoked. You have twenty-four hours to clean out your office and vacate the premises. And I'll remind you, if you ever speak a word about any of what you've seen at this facility, you'll be found guilty of treason. Punishable by death."

"Mechanized infantry!" the General commanded. "Remove the doctor from the floor. And return Subject Two to his cell."

"Removing," the robots confirmed. "Returning."

A robot hoisted Miles from the table.

The General leveled a deadly stare at him. "You have twenty-four hours, boy. Tell me everything about being Gilded, or pay the price. Dismissed."

CHAPTER 19

MILES BARELY REMEMBERED THE TRIP BACK TO HIS cell. Between the knockout drug, the truth concoction, and whatever the doctor had given him to counteract it, his brain was mush. He flopped onto his cot and curled into a ball. He must've been unconscious much longer than he thought, because when he came to, the lights were dimmed for bedtime.

"Miles?" Henry whispered in the dark.

"Leave me alone."

"Are you okay? Where did they take you?"

The cell was spinning. "I'm serious. I don't feel like talking."

Maybe Henry just wanted more details to add to his mental database of the prison, but none of that mattered anymore. If Miles didn't come up with a way out by tomorrow, the General was going to follow through on his threats.

Miles looked around his cell. Nothing but the cot

and the chair. Was that all his life was going to be from now on? Sitting up or lying down, spending every waking moment thinking about how his failures had hurt his friends and family?

Miles stood, and the cell spun worse. He reached out to steady himself and flopped onto the chair. Luckily it was sturdy and metal.

Sturdy. Metal. His first day in the cell, Miles had swung this same chair at the glass wall as hard as he could. The glass door hadn't been damaged in the least.

And neither had the chair.

A plan started to form. Not really a plan, so much as an idea. A kernel of an idea. At best.

It was risky. It was crazy. But it just might work.

One way or another, this was Miles's last day as a prisoner. Either they were going to escape, or he'd die in the attempt. There was no other option.

Oh-seven-hundred loomed like high noon in one of those Western movies Mr. Taylor liked to watch: ominous, dangerous, and final.

Miles had barely slept, so flip-jittery were his nerves. He'd have to be quick. He'd have to be strong. He'd have to be heroic.

What he was, was scared.

Quick. Strong. Heroic. All qualities Miles possessed when he wore the cape. But he'd botched that.

The General had the cape hidden somewhere in the base, and for all Miles knew, Breckenridge was hell-bent on unraveling it one thread at a time until he could make it do what he desired. Miles's encounter with the General the day before had only affirmed what he already feared was true but had been unwilling to admit—his time as Gilded was over.

He'd never forgive himself for ruining the best thing that had ever happened to him. Maybe Henry wouldn't either. But he needed to push that out of his mind now. It was time for him to salvage the only thing he could: their freedom.

Oh-seven-hundred finally arrived, and the day's routine began. Corporal Jerry escorted Miles and Henry to breakfast. A pair of battle robots brought Lenore soon after.

Miles couldn't touch his food, and not because it was onions. He was nervous, tension stretching his insides like a drum.

"Miles?" Henry was studying him with concern. "I know you don't want to talk about what they did in the lab, but it's important." Henry's voice dropped to a whisper. "There's a weak spot in their routine. I know there is. And I'm going to find it."

Miles shot a glance at Lenore. The mention of the lab seemed to make her lose her appetite, too. "I can't explain why, Henry, but we need to get out of here. Today."

Henry's voice was filled with concern. "That isn't a good idea. We need a plan first. We need to be patient."

"I already have a plan," Miles whispered. "When Jerry takes us back to our cells, get his attention. Scream your head off. Throw a fit. I don't care what. Just do it."

"Whoa. Let's talk this through. What're you—"

"You have to trust me," Miles said. He glanced at the robots guarding the door. "Please. It has to be today. Just nod if you're with me."

Lenore nodded. Henry did, too, but Miles could tell he didn't like being in the dark.

After breakfast and cleanup time, Jerry escorted Miles and Henry back to the their cells. Lenore gave Miles a nervous glance as he walked by.

Miles steeled himself. He had a tiny window of opportunity. But it was the only window he had.

Jerry scanned his keycard past the lock on Miles's cell, and the glass wall whisked upward. Miles backed over the threshold, exchanging a glance with Henry. Miles could tell Henry understood.

Go time.

Jerry reached out to wave his keycard in front of the lock and seal Miles inside.

"Jerry . . . ?" Henry said weakly.

Jerry's hand stopped, and he looked back over his shoulder at Henry. "What is it?"

"I—I don't feel so . . . so . . . AUGH!" Henry dropped to the floor, hands grabbing his stomach like he'd swallowed broken glass. He was threatening the one thing that is 100 percent guaranteed to freak out every adult in the room: kid puke.

It was genius.

"Whoa!" Jerry blurted. "Don't throw up, kid!"

Miles crept toward his cell's steel chair. He was a powder keg of adrenaline ready to explode, but he had to keep his cool. If he made the slightest sound, they were sunk.

Henry writhed, moaning louder. "AAAUUUGLL!"

"It's the onions!" Jerry blurted. "I warned the General to lay off, but he gets them free from the farm down South. He never listens to me!" Jerry scooped up Henry by one arm, trying to get him to stand.

Miles hoisted the chair by two legs like a war club.

Henry went limp like his bones were noodles, pulling Jerry down with him. "It's coming up!"

"Not yet! Not yet!" Jerry urged. "Get to the toilet!"

Miles crept forward. He held the chair high, taking aim at the back of Jerry's head. He was going to get only one shot at this. It had to count.

Just as he was about to swing, he caught sight of his reflection in the glass wall of Henry's cell. And there, right beside it, Miles saw Jerry's narrow eyes glaring back at him.

Uh-oh.

"Oh, no, you don't!" Jerry wailed.

Jerry fumbled for his gun. Miles mustered all his strength and swung for a knockout blow.

Jerry yelped and dodged. He wasn't fast, but he was fast enough. The chair missed him by an inch, sailing from Miles's hands and clattering to the ground.

Miles and Jerry stood and stared at each other, as if neither knew what to do next. Then Jerry broke the silence. "You'll have to do better than that to escape from *me*," he gloated.

"CHARGE!" Henry leaped onto Jerry's back. He smacked his hands over Jerry's eyes, blinding him.

Jerry bucked and spun. "This is insubordination!"

Henry hung on like a rodeo man riding a bucking bull. "Help!" he hollered.

"How?" Miles hollered back.

"I don't know!"

Miles went with his gut. He rushed Jerry from behind, planting his shoulder into the small of his back and shoving as hard as he could. Jerry stumbled forward, pumping his legs to keep his feet under him.

Henry sprang clear. Jerry had just enough time to glimpse the glass wall of an empty cell before pasting his face against it like a plump dove colliding with a window.

THUNNNG!

Miles stepped back and caught his breath, steeling himself for Jerry's counterattack. Henry stood in a karate pose, even though—as far as Miles knew—he didn't know a lick of martial arts.

Jerry teetered for a moment, then slid down the glass wall, his lips leaving behind a trail of slobber.

He'd knocked himself out cold.

"*This* was your plan?" Henry said, exasperated.

"Later!" Miles said urgently. "Get the keycard!"

"Right!"

They rolled Jerry onto his back, and Miles slipped the lanyard off his neck. He swiped the keycard past the lock outside Lenore's cell. "You were supposed to help with the distracting!"

Lenore stepped out. "I didn't want to steal Henry's thunder. That was really . . . something." She looked down at her feet planted on the concrete outside her cell. Then she grinned. "No restraints."

"Don't celebrate yet. We still have to find a way out of this place."

Then an alarm blared, and the chase was on.

CHAPTER 20

BACKING UP THE ALARM WAS A REPEATED message in an automated voice. "Containment breach. Mechanized infantry to the cells . . . Containment breach. Mechanized infantry to the cells . . ."

Miles swiped the keycard to unlock the vault door that opened to the hallway. "Run!"

"Where are we going?" Henry panted.

"The General said this was the prison level. That means there has to be other levels." Miles was terrified. They'd been free for less than thirty seconds, and he was already doubting himself. "There's got to be stairs somewhere."

"I know the way!" Lenore cut in. "The robots have led me past a stairwell a few times. Follow me!"

They turned right, and Lenore stopped short. Miles and Henry had to skid to keep from plowing into her.

Farther down the hall a trio of battle robots waited.

They each cycled through their tool assortment and produced a restraint loop like the one Miles had seen them use on Lenore.

"Halt," the robots droned.

Lenore turned to Miles and Henry. She was deadly serious. "Do you trust me?"

Jerry turned the corner in the direction they'd run from. Miles had been in such a rush, he'd neglected to close the vault door and seal Jerry inside. Now they were trapped, enemies in front and behind them.

"STOFF THEM!" Jerry shouted, his hands cradling his smashed nose.

"Do you trust me?" Lenore repeated.

"Is there a choice?" Miles answered.

"Then get behind me and stay there!"

Lenore bolted, and Miles and Henry followed. Miles noticed she had an odd, loping gate, as if she were trying to touch as little of the ground as possible. Whatever the reason, she was fast.

"Incoming attack detected," the robots stated. "Advancing." The robots lurched forward.

"Don't charge!" Jerry screamed. "Stand your ground!"

The robots ignored him and continued forward.

Twenty feet.

Ten.

Escape or die trying. That was the promise Miles made himself. He hunched his head down into his shoulders and waited for the crunch of metal against his skull.

BOING!

Last time Miles had heard that sound, Henry had ended up sprawled on the cafeteria floor. Now, it was the robots' turn. He looked back over his shoulder and saw the robots were already behind them, flailing on the ground like turned-over turtles. Miles didn't understand how someone of Lenore's size was able to bowl over three thousand pounds of death metal, but if Coach Lineman had seen it, the Jammer might've found himself playing backup to the only girl linebacker in Georgia.

Henry blinked at Lenore. "You . . . ? How . . . ?"

"Security! Security!" Jerry shouted shrilly to no one in particular. "They're getting away!"

They ran. Down hallways and around corners, they ran. Each time they encountered another squad of robots, they ducked into another hallway. Miles felt like a mouse who'd escaped his cage only to find himself lost in a maze. But Lenore never slowed her pace. She'd been a prisoner so long, she seemed to have the whole place memorized. Miles felt bad for her and was thankful for her at the same time.

Finally, they came to a stairwell. Miles swiped the keycard, and they fell through the door just as a pair of robots turned the corner behind them.

Miles checked the stairwell. In both directions, concrete steps disappeared into shadow. "Which way?"

"I'm not sure," Lenore said. "They never took me off the prison level."

Henry was already in motion. "Up! Secret bases are always underground!"

It was as good a guess as any. They bounded up the steps. Two flights. A third. Henry stopped on the fourth landing, craning his ear upward. "Shhh!"

The sounds of treaded feet grinding over stairs echoed from above.

Henry snatched the keycard from Miles. "Exit! Exit!" He swiped the keycard next to a door marked with an *L*. They dove through and locked the door behind them.

"We can't go back in the stairwell," Miles whispered. "We need to find another way up."

They crept past open doorways, but none of them had keycard locks. The rooms looked like offices, but there wasn't anyone inside them. Papers were scattered on the floors, lunches left half eaten. Everything looked evacuated.

"This is an administrative level or something," Henry said. "When the alarm went off, everyone must have cleared out." Then he looked at Lenore. "That was a pretty neat trick you pulled back there."

Miles was confused. "What trick?"

"You didn't see it? The way the robots—"

Lenore stopped walking. "There's a reason they locked me up in here. You don't want to know what it is."

Henry raised his hands, showing Lenore his palms. "You don't have to be scared. We all have secrets." Henry stepped closer, reaching out slowly. "And your secret is safe with us."

Miles felt like he was four years old, eavesdropping on the grown-ups' table during Thanksgiving and having not the foggiest idea what they were talking about. "Can we have sharing time later? We're kind of in the middle of a jailbreak here."

"I know why the General locked you up," Henry continued, ignoring Miles. "He thinks there's something wrong with you. That you're dangerous."

Lenore eyed Henry's hand. It was just about to touch her shoulder. "Don't," she warned.

Henry's hand settled softly on her. "You're not dangerous. You're just different."

Lenore stared in amazement at Henry's hand. "How'd you know?"

"I didn't at first. It took some observation to piece it together. Seeing what you did to those robots finally connected the dots."

Miles was frustrated and feeling a little left out. "What's everyone talking about?"

"You won't tell anyone if we get out of here, will

you?" Lenore asked. "Enough people treat me like a freak as it is."

"Never." Henry squeezed her shoulder for emphasis. "If there are two people in the world you can count on, they're Miles and me."

"Miles and I," Lenore said, smiling tightly.

"Touché." Henry smiled back. "And if you want my opinion, 'Skip' would make a pretty awesome superhero name."

"Someone tell me what's going on here!" Miles blurted.

"Yes," a voice spoke up. "I'd like to know the same thing."

Miles almost jumped out of his jumpsuit. All three of them spun around to discover a woman in a white lab coat looking back at them. She had a touch tablet in one hand and a stylus in the other, like she was ready to jot down whatever answer they gave her.

Miles recognized her. It was the doctor, the one from the lab. "You."

"Her," Lenore breathed.

"Dr. Petri?" Henry said, awed. "Dr. Marisol Petri?"

The doctor cocked an eyebrow. "That's correct."

"I'm a huge fan of your work!" Henry was jubilant. "Your paper on the potential genetic link between the duck-billed platypus and extraterrestrial mammals was inspiring!" He stepped forward with an extended hand.

Lenore clutched Henry's arm. "Stay away from her," she warned. "She works for the General."

Henry jabbed a thumb at Dr. Petri. "Her? No way. She's the most respected mind in her field."

Lenore was getting more freaked out by the second. "I don't care. She does all the tests. Once a week since I got here. She's evil."

"It's not what you think," Dr. Petri said guiltily. "I . . . I was helping you. Making sure you were healthy."

"You want to keep us in cages so you can experiment on us like animals!" Lenore was furious. "You do whatever the General tells you, and you think *we're* a danger to people."

Miles stepped forward. "You did all that?"

Dr. Petri stared at the ground. "It isn't that simple. The General is a very powerful man. He wouldn't let me quit. He doesn't need a cell to keep someone captive." She gazed at Miles with a heartfelt look in her eyes. "If I could take it all back, I would."

"You're a liar!" Lenore screamed.

"Lenore, wait. She might be telling the truth. When the General was interrogating me, she barged in and put a stop to it. She stood up to him. I saw it."

BABOOOM!

The sound of an explosion rippled down the hallway like an earthquake.

"The robots blew the door," Henry whined. "They're coming."

Miles glared at Dr. Petri. "If you really want to make up for what you've done, help us. We can all get out of here together."

For a moment Dr. Petri seemed not to know what to do. Then she locked her jaw. "To heck with this," she said. "Follow me." She turned and hurried down the hall.

Miles turned to Lenore and Henry. "She's our best shot."

They chased after Dr. Petri, who ducked into a lab and began tapping at a screen on the wall. There were half-filled boxes of medicals texts and lab equipment on the floor.

"I didn't sign up for this," she grumbled to herself. "I'm not some mad scientist."

She seemed pretty mad to Miles.

"Um, Doctor?" Henry offered, glancing at the screen. "I have nothing but the utmost respect for you, and under any other circumstance, I'd be thrilled to go over your research. But right now we need to get out of here."

"He doesn't get to have it," she muttered, lost in her own train of thought. "Everything I did for him. He said I'd be studying the aftereffects of the extraterrestrial invasion on the local populace."

Images of X-rays and others scans flashed over the

screen. A boy Miles's size. A girl shaped like Lenore. Another boy, smaller than the others.

Miles didn't need to be a theoretical zoologist to understand what he was seeing. "That's . . . Those are us."

Dr. Petri looked sorry and angry at the same time. "Yes. But the General can kiss all of my findings good-bye. What he never knew is that I programmed a security loophole into my research files. After I've transferred them to my device, I can wipe them from the base's system. Medical dossiers, lab results, test data—everything. Names and personal information, too. It'll be like you were never here."

Henry glanced uneasily toward the door. "How long is this going to take?"

"Only another minute."

Out in the hallway, the pounding of boots drew closer.

"Hide!" Dr. Petri whispered.

Miles dove behind the desk. Lenore slid behind a tall filing cabinet, pressing her back against the wall. Henry stuffed himself into a storage unit filled with beakers and test tubes.

The heavy footsteps pounded closer, then plodded into the office.

"Hi . . . Dr. . . . Petri." Jerry was panting and short of breath.

"What can I do for you, Jerry?"

"This level . . . is supposed to be . . . evacuated."

"I was finishing packing my things, like the General told me to. Is something wrong?"

"Have you . . . seen anything out of . . . the ordinary?"

"Oh, sure." Dr. Petri feigned obliviousness. "Once I saw the fossilized skeleton of an apatosaurus with two heads."

"I mean . . . have you seen anything . . . today. Anything . . . unexpected."

"No. But there's been a lot of noise on the level. It's more than a little distracting."

"All right." Jerry groaned. He jogged from the office, taking his heavy footsteps with him.

Miles poked his head out from behind the desk. "Can we go now?"

Dr. Petri studied her tablet, then nodded. "You better believe it."

Lenore stepped out from behind the filing cabinet, and Henry unfolded himself from inside the storage unit. "Have you really seen a two-headed apatosaurus?" he asked.

"I have. And why do I get the feeling that's nothing compared to the things you three have seen? Now, let's get to the elevator."

CHAPTER 21

THEY PILED INTO AN ELEVATOR JUST DOWN THE HALL.

Dr. Petri reached for a button with the letter *G* on it. There were six other buttons. One of them was red, and there was a keycard lock beside it.

Miles stopped Dr. Petri's hand. He pointed at the red button. "What's that one?"

"Level zero," Dr. Petri answered. "The lowest section of the underground complex. I've never been down there. General Breckenridge is very fond of reminding me that it's classified."

Miles and Henry exchanged a glance. "There must be something really secret down there," Miles said. "Like, more secret than testing on live children."

Dr. Petri frowned at the lock. "We'll just have to wonder. Without the right ID card, we can't get to the lower levels."

"You mean like this one?" Henry held up Jerry's card.

Dr. Petri nodded. "Just like that one."

Miles had a hunch so deep down in his bones, he knew it was true. "It's the cape. It has to be down there."

Miles had blown his chances of ever wearing the cape again, but he could still make sure it had an opportunity to find someone worthy. It was like Henry had told him—he was part of a grand and noble legacy. A hero's legacy. No matter the cost, that legacy had to continue.

Miles wished his time with the cape had been longer. For that he had only himself to blame. But in the end he was satisfied. And besides, Miles Taylor, Former Superhero, was still a pretty cool title. Even if the world would never know the things he'd done, it didn't matter. He knew. And he was proud.

"Henry, give me the card. After you guys get to the surface, I'll go back down. I can't leave. Not yet."

Henry's fingers tightened on the card. "Nice try."

"I'm serious. All the stuff you said about me wanting bad things to happen so I could be a hero? It's all true. I get that now. This isn't about me not being able to let go of Gilded. The cape doesn't belong locked up in some basement somewhere. And it certainly doesn't belong to General Breckenridge. It belongs to the world. I've got to get it back."

Henry nodded. "You're right. That's why I'm going

down there with you. We're a team, remember? You stay, I stay."

"*We* stay," Lenore stressed. She cracked her knuckles against the palm of her hand. "You two need all the help you can get."

Miles turned to Dr. Petri. "Are you in or out?"

Dr. Petri was resolute. "I can't abandon you kids here alone. I should've stood up to Breckenridge a long time ago. If this is my chance to make good, I won't run from it."

Miles clenched his fists. "Okay. Let's finish this."

Henry swiped the keycard past the lock, and the red button lit up. "Here we go." He pressed it, and the elevator car began to drop.

Down two levels.

Down three.

Miles felt as though he were lowering himself into the belly of a huge monster, one he'd never be able to climb back out of. Everything they'd done to escape and get as far as they had—so close to finally being free—and they were throwing it all away for what was most likely an express ticket back to their cells. Or an early grave. As worried as Miles was about the others, he was thankful not to be alone.

The elevator stopped with a cheery *ding!* Instead of the front doors opening, the rear of the car slid back. What Miles saw next made him catch his breath.

A war zone. Or what was left of one. And indoor, to boot.

They were in a vast, concrete bunker the length of a football field, and maybe as tall, too. The walls stretched up until they disappeared into gloom. It wasn't just the lowest level of the complex. It was the height of all the other levels combined, positioned beside them to double the size of the facility.

The floor and walls were gouged with deep grooves, scorched from the heat of fires and pockmarked with thousands of holes of various sizes.

Positioned throughout the bunker were weapons of every type and design. A rack holding rifles, chain guns, and flamethrowers. Rows of grenade launchers, mortars, and howitzers. Even a full-blown tank parked off to the side, complete with a camouflage paint job that did absolutely nothing to hide it in its current surroundings.

The walls had to be thick to withstand all the damage those armaments could dish out. Miles suddenly found it hard to breathe, like he'd stepped into a tomb. The world's biggest, most heavily armed tomb.

Henry whistled. "Looks like World War III happened in here."

"Split up," Miles said. "We'll cover more ground."

"What exactly are we searching for?" Dr. Petri asked.

"Ummm," Miles stammered. "See, it's kind of gold colored . . . and it looks like a blanket . . . and—"

"Gilded's cape," Lenore said. "Miles here puts on the cape, and he turns into a superhero."

If Dr. Petri was surprised, she did a good job of hiding it. "So you're the one who lives up off Jimmy Carter Boulevard."

Miles looked to Henry for guidance. "How should I answer?"

Dr. Petri was matter-of-fact. "If it puts you at ease, I can keep information confidential. I've spent the past year dissecting extraterrestrials for the United States government. My head is filled with things the world will never see or hear about." She paused, considering her last statement. "Hopefully."

Henry shrugged. "I guess she's good. So let's find the cape."

Just then the floor started to tremble. A deafening noise filled the room, like the grinding of a million heavy gears.

"Where's it coming from?" Miles shouted.

Henry pointed skyward. "Take cover!"

They scrambled behind the biggest thing they could find—the tank. Miles looked up and watched with horror as a massive metal grate lowered out of the shadows above, carried downward by cables as thick as telephone poles.

Lenore jammed her fingers into her ears. "What is it?"

"Must be how all the hardware got down here!" Henry answered. "You can't fit a howitzer on an elevator!"

As the metal grate got closer. Miles spied tripod legs and arms and eye beams he recognized all too well—battle robots. Rows and rows of them arranged in ranks. Miles realized with dread that the mere handful he'd encountered up until this point was just one small part of a far more terrifying fighting force. An army like this could mulch anyone who stood against them beneath its cold, metal treads. Anyone except a superhero. Maybe. Too bad there wasn't one of those around to find out.

The grate touched down. Miles peered around the nose of the tank. Puffed up with pride at the forefront of his diabolical army was General Breckenridge. He'd traded in his formal uniform and shoes for combat fatigues and boots, as though he knew a war was coming and he wanted to dress the part.

Jerry stood behind him, toeing the ground ruefully. He looked like he'd just received the worst scolding of his thoroughly scolded military career.

The General's voice went off like a bomb burst. "Mechanized infantry! Attack pattern omega! Hold fire and await my command!"

"Executing attack pattern omega, General Breckenridge," the robots confirmed. They rolled forward and spread out, enclosing Miles and the others in a wide arc. They raised their cannon arms and flipped through their tool assortments, producing sharp bayonets two feet long. "Holding fire and awaiting the General's command."

The General stepped from the grate, his hands behind his back. The grate lifted into the blackness again. "I have you surrounded. Even if you could reach the elevator alive—which you can't—I've deauthorized the keycard you have in your possession. It's no longer operational." He glowered at Jerry, his eyes hot coals. "For anyone."

Jerry tucked his head into his shoulders.

The General smiled, a thin crack splitting his stone-hard face. "This need not resort to bloodshed. I implore you to spare your own lives and do the sensible thing: surrender."

"You don't really think he'll fire on us, do you?" Dr. Petri asked.

"Oh, he'll most definitely fire on us," Henry said grimly. "You see the walls of this place? We're dealing with one trigger-happy man."

Lenore clenched her teeth. "What do we do?"

"I'm thinking," Miles said, wishing they had options and knowing they didn't. There was only one thing in all the world—maybe even the universe—that could save them.

The General sneered. "I know what you're thinking." He voiced it with such confidence, Miles wondered if he'd reached into Miles's mind and pulled out his thoughts. "You believe you can still reclaim this."

General Breckenridge brought his hands out from behind his back. Lying across them, folded into a tight triangle like a ceremonial flag, was the cape.

Good news: Miles had found the cape.

Bad news: To get it back, he'd have to beat an army of mechanical killers led by a power-mad military commander.

They were done for.

CHAPTER 22

HOW HAD IT COME TO THIS?

Actually, Miles knew exactly how it'd come to this. He'd broken nearly every single rule of being Gilded. The only rule he hadn't broken was . . .

Nope. He'd broken them all.

General Breckenridge unfolded the cape. Seeing his hands all over it made Miles see red. He stepped out from behind the tank. "The cape isn't yours!" he shouted.

"Miles!" Henry called. "Get back here!"

Miles heard the concern in Henry's voice, but he was too furious to care. He pointed accusingly at the General. "You stole it!"

The General cocked his head to the side, considering Miles's words. "Spoils of war. I earned this cape through patience, leadership, and strategy. Which makes me far more worthy than if an onion farmer had given it to me by happenstance in a parking garage."

Miles fumed. "At least I know how it works. When I find the right person to wear it, I'll teach them. But that person won't ever be you. Passing the cape on is the only responsibility I have left. I won't mess that up, too."

"You really are a child." The General wrinkled his nose, as though the word had an unpleasant odor. "So naive. What do you know of responsibility? You're thirteen. A quarter of your life was spent peeing into a diaper.

"It's difficult to fathom such immeasurable power in the possession of a mere child. No military training. No discipline. No illustrious career spent preparing for desperate moments. It's disconcerting."

Miles inched closer to the General. If he could just get within reach . . .

The General was fixated on the cape, his fingers caressing it. "I started by trying to cut the corner with a knife. The blade broke. So I tried a pistol, then a rifle, then a bazooka."

So many robots had their cannons and bayonets pointed at Miles. His feet felt like a thousand pounds of wet lead. Somehow, he dragged them two steps closer.

The General turned, gesturing sweepingly at the bunker. "Then the flamethrowers, the howitzers, and even the tank. Look at what they did to the room. But the cape"—the General held it close, its golden glow reflected in his eyes—"the cape remains perfect."

Miles stopped cold.

"It's glowing," Henry breathed, echoing Miles's thoughts. "Why's it glowing for him?"

"I remember the first time I saw it up close," the General said, draping the cape over his shoulders. "The day those foul alien invaders attacked us. That was a desperate moment indeed. If not for this remarkable weapon, all would've been lost."

Miles had an awful feeling.

The General grabbed one half of the cape's clasp in each hand. "If that were to happen again, who'd keep the country safe?"

Despair. That was the feeling washing over Miles. Complete, abject despair.

The General dropped the cape over his shoulders and brought the clasp halves closer. "What if a worse enemy comes? That would be such a desperate moment, only a true hero would be able to prevail."

Miles watched with horror as the clasp halves came closer. They wanted to join together. They wanted to be whole.

He wanted to sob.

It wasn't possible. It could never be. The General was—

...GILDED?
2305121

UM, HENRY? GENERAL BRECKENRIDGE IS THE *BAD GUY* HERE, RIGHT?
DEFINITELY.

SO WHY DOES HE LOOK LIKE THE *GOOD GUY?!*

AN INTERESTING QUESTION. I DON'T RECALL EVIDENCE OF AN EVENT LIKE THIS OCCURRING BEFORE.

I WONDER--
HENRY.
--IF THE CAPE'S INTERNAL ASSESSMENT ALGORITHM--
HENRY!

STOP *INTERRUPTING!* YOU WANT MY *EDUCATED GUESS* OR NOT!

LOOK OUT!

GAZE UPON YOUR NEW *HERO!*
OH. *RIGHT.*

I POSSESS A HERO'S MIGHT!
KRRNCH
A HERO'S PHYSIQUE!
AND THE ULTIMATE HERO'S UNIFORM!

THIS IS WHAT I WAS BORN FOR. I'LL BE THE GREATEST HERO HISTORY HAS EVER WITNESSED.
WHENEVER A DESPERATE MOMENT ARRIVES, I'LL BE THERE!

MILES! YOU KNOW THE CAPE BETTER THAN ANYONE. YOU KNOW WHAT MAKES IT WORK.
AND WHAT MAKES IT NOT WORK.

RIGHT...

I'LL GIVE IT TO YOU, GENERAL. THE UNIFORM REALLY DOES SUIT YOU.
I CAN TELL YOU'VE BEEN TRAINING FOR THIS YOUR WHOLE LIFE. GUESS YOU DON'T NEED JERRY ANYMORE.
SORRY, JERRY.
SIGH

OR YOUR ROBOT ARMY.
THUMP THUMP
I MEAN, NOW THAT YOU HAVE THE CAPE, WHAT'S THE POINT OF SHARING YOUR GLORY WITH A BUNCH OF MACHINES?

YOU LACK A MILITARY MIND, BOY.
I CAN'T BE IN ALL PLACES AT ALL TIMES. NOT EVEN AS GILDED. BUT MY MECHANIZED INFANTRY...

...THEY'LL BE AN UNERRING EXTENSION OF MY WILL. ACTING ONLY UNDER MY DIRECT ORDERS.
EVERYONE WILL KNOW I CREATED THEM.
THAT I'M NOT JUST A SUPERHERO, BUT A BATTLEFIELD GENIUS AS WELL.

AFTER ALL, WHAT GOOD IS AN ARMY, IF YOU DON'T USE IT?

GUESS YOU HAVE IT ALL FIGURED OUT, THEN. COME ON, EVERYONE. LET'S HEAD BACK TO THE CELLS.
DOC, I HOPE YOU AREN'T ALLERGIC TO ONIONS.
MILES? WHAT ARE YOU DOING?

BUT WAIT. THERE'S JUST ONE TINY THING YOU HAVEN'T THOUGHT OF, GENERAL.
WHAT'S THAT?
YEAH, WHAT'S THAT?

ME.

YOU BELIEVE YOU CAN POSE A THREAT TO MY PLANS? ABSURD.
YOU THOUGHT THAT WHEN YOU BROUGHT ME HERE, DIDN'T YOU? BUT I ESCAPED YOUR JAIL AND COULD'VE MADE IT ALL THE WAY OUT.
YOU DIDN'T EXPECT THAT, I BET.

OH, SURE. TAKE ALL THE CREDIT.
HENRY?
SHUT. UP.

AND YOU'RE FORGETTING THE MOST IMPORTANT DETAIL, GENERAL: I'M THE ONLY OTHER PERSON ALIVE TO HAVE WORN THE CAPE.
I WORE IT FOR A WHOLE YEAR. WHICH MEANS I KNOW A HECK OF A LOT MORE ABOUT IT THAN YOU.
THAT GOES DOUBLE FOR HENRY. HE'S NEVER WORN THE CAPE AT ALL, BUT HE UNDERSTANDS IT EVEN BETTER THAN ME.

THAT'S MORE LIKE IT.

KEEPING US ALIVE IS JUST BAD STRATEGY.

YOU CAN STOP GIVING ME CREDIT NOW!

COME TO THINK OF IT, LENORE AND DOCTOR PETRI ARE A PROBLEM, TOO.
I MEAN, THE MOST IMPORTANT RULE OF BEING GILDED IS NOT LETTING ANYONE KNOW YOUR REAL IDENTITY. AND WE ALL KNOW WHO YOU ARE.
YOU SHOULD PROBABLY GET RID OF US, JUST TO BE SAFE.

STOP TALKING!
HE ISN'T BIG ON THINKING THINGS THROUGH, IS HE?
THIS IS THE STRANGEST DAY I'VE EVER HAD.

YOU...YOU'RE CORRECT.
YOU DO KNOW MORE ABOUT THE CAPE. YOU DO KNOW WHO I AM.
AND I CAN TAKE IT ALL AWAY FROM YOU.

I'LL SEE ABOUT THAT.
UH-OH.

AAAAAH!

WHOA! WHOA! WHOA! LET'S TALK ABOUT THIS ON THE GROUND!
THINK YOU CAN TAKE THE CAPE FROM ME?
FROM ME?

I WAITED MY ENTIRE LIFE TO BE A HERO!
I'LL NEVER LOSE IT!

HISTORY BOOKS WILL DEDICATE WHOLE CHAPTERS TO ME! GAME SHOWS WILL ASK TRIVIA ABOUT ME!
I'LL BE ADORED AND ADMIRED BY ALL!

DON'T SAY "IMAGINE THE GLORY!" DON'T SAY "IMAGINE THE GLORY!"

IMAGINE THE GLORY!

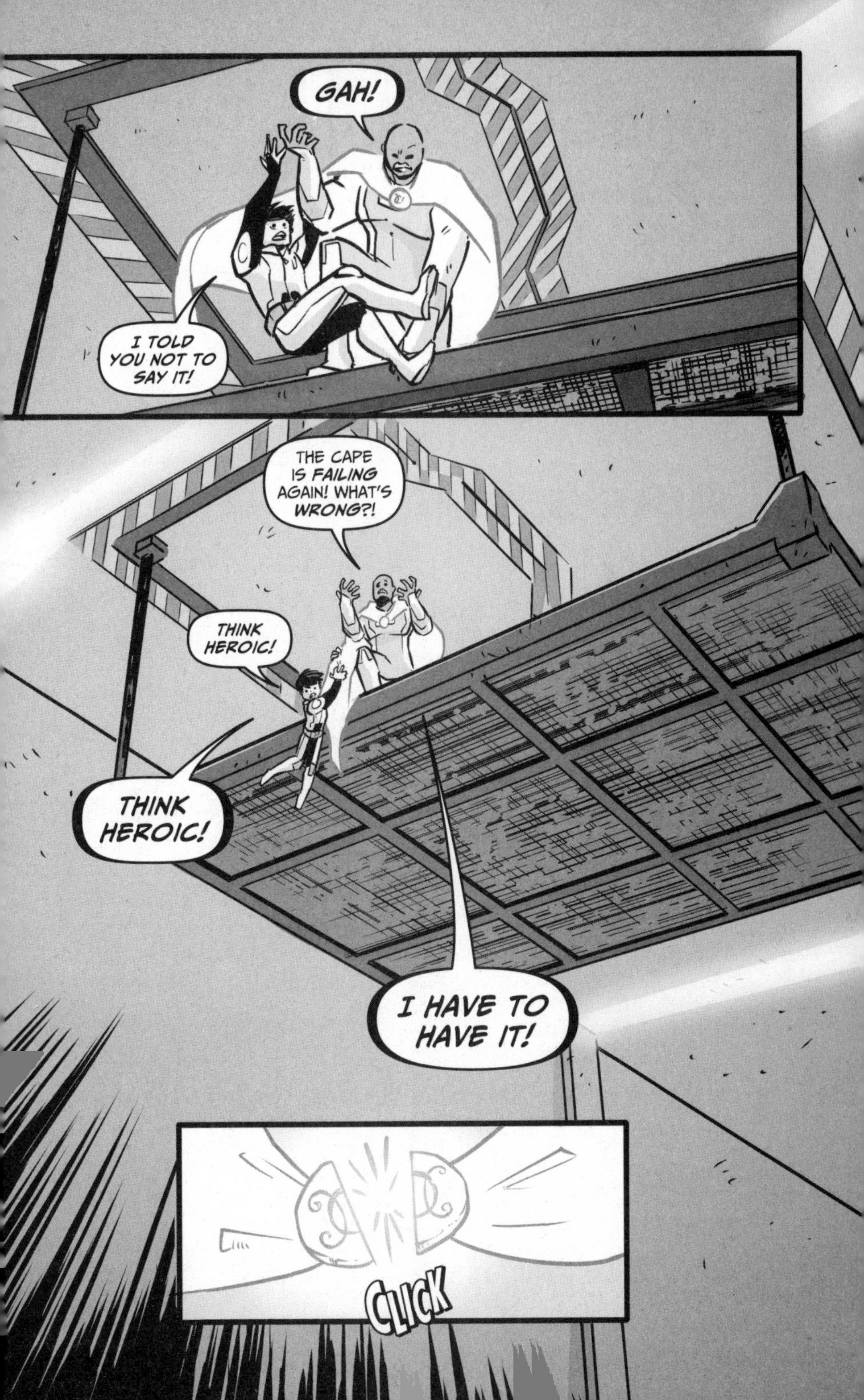
GAH!
I TOLD YOU NOT TO SAY IT!
THE CAPE IS FAILING AGAIN! WHAT'S WRONG?!
THINK HEROIC!
THINK HEROIC!
I HAVE TO HAVE IT!
CLICK

CHAPTER 23

MILES KNEW HE WAS DEAD.

Unless . . .

The cape was clutched in his fingers.

He fumbled with the clasp,

somersaulting and spinning downward.

Downward.

He somehow pulled the cape over his shoulders

and touched the clasp together.

Nothing.

He didn't want to die.

But not wanting to die wasn't enough.

He made a silent vow only the cape could hear.

Let me make it right.

One chance to save my friends.

I'll never ask to be a hero again.

WOOOOHOOOO!

OH, YEAH!
MECHANIZED INFANTRY! KILL GILDED!
GET THAT CAPE!
KILLING GILDED, GENERAL BRECKENRIDGE.
OH, NO...

CHBOOM!
CHBOOM!
CHBOOM!

KRAKOOM

BAYONET CHARGE!

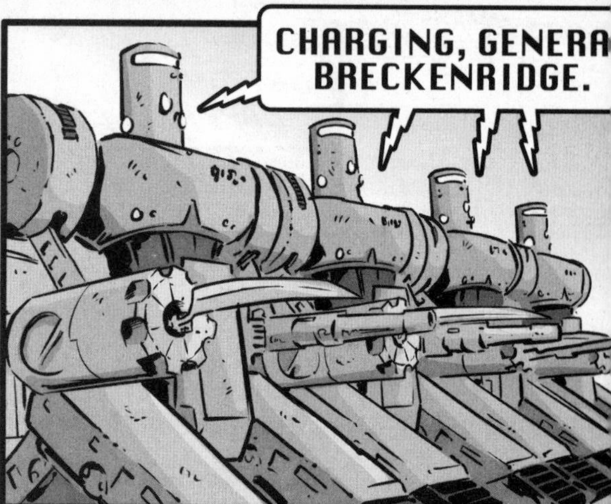
CHARGING, GENERA
BRECKENRIDGE.

NNNGH

KRRANG

KRUNNG

JUST KEEP FIGHTING, DON'T YOU?

SO DO I!
ZZZNT

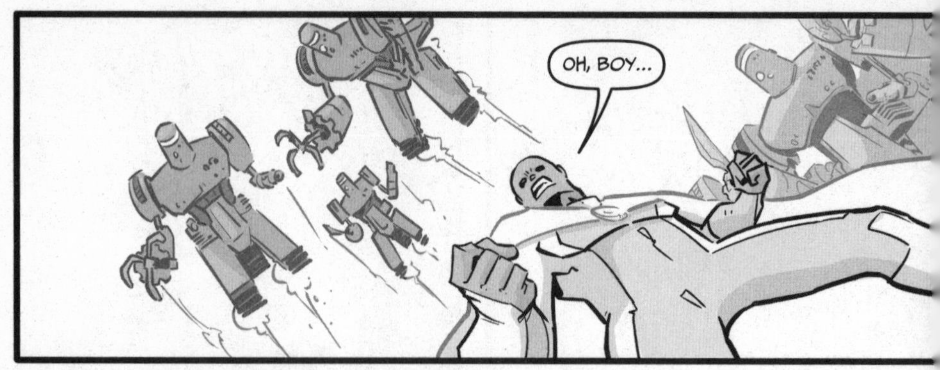
OH, BOY...

THERE'S *TOO MANY*! HE CAN'T BEAT THEM BY HIMSELF!

LET GO!

WE HAVE TO *HELP*!
I'M NOT GOING BACK IN A CAGE. I *WON'T*.

OONF

HELP!

AAAAGH!

THERE'S NO USE STRUGGLING. MY MECHANIZED INFANTRY WERE CREATED TO WITHSTAND THE *HARSHEST* ADVERSARIES. ALL MY YEARS OF MILITARY EXPERIENCE DISTILLED INTO THE *PERFECT* ARMY.

YOU *WILL* RELINQUISH THE CAPE AND TELL ME EVERYTHING YOU KNOW ABOUT IT. YOU AREN'T QUALIFIED TO BE THE HERO THE WORLD REQUIRES. LEAVE THE *DESPERATE MOMENTS* TO ME.

FORGET IT!

FRIENDS.

CHILDREN.

SECOND PLATOON! GET THEM!
GETTING THEM, GENERAL BRECKENRIDGE.

SKIP! YOU'RE UP!

STOP! IT'S TOO DANGEROUS!
SHE CAN HANDLE THIS, DOCTOR.
I HOPE.

CHBOOM!
CHBOOM!

YOU CAN'T HURT ME.
TCK
TCK

CHBOOM!
CHBOOM!

YOU WON'T TOUCH ME.
TCK
TCK

YOU'LL NEVER LOCK ME UP AGAIN!
KA-THWAM

BABOOM
AGH!

KRAKANG

ALL MY TESTING... I'M AWARE OF WHAT LENORE CAN DO, BUT I'VE NEVER SEEN HER UNLEASHED UNTIL NOW. SHE'S *REMARKABLE*.
IT TOOK ME A WHILE TO UNDERSTAND IT.

LENORE HAS A *PROTECTIVE FIELD* AROUND HER, RIGHT?
ANYTHING MOVING AT *HIGH VELOCITY* CAN'T GET THROUGH--SORT OF LIKE A ROCK SKIPPING OFF THE SURFACE OF A LAKE.
IT WORKS THE SAME WAY WHEN *SHE'S* MOVING FAST, WHICH I GUESS IN THOSE INSTANCES WOULD MAKE HER THE ROCK? I'M NOT SURE. I'M STILL FIGURING IT OUT. MAYBE IF--

WE'LL TALK ABOUT IT MORE IF WE *SURVIVE*!
RIGHT! *FOLLOW ME!*

NYAAH!

INCOMING!
THWABAM

THAT WAS SO COOL!
I KNOW, RIGHT? HIGH FIVE!

WHA--?
TCK

GOTCHA.

WHAT ARE WE LOOKING FOR?
NOT WHAT! WHO!

JERRY! ORDER THE ROBOTS TO STOP SHOOTING! DON'T MAKE ME USE MY MOVES ON YOU!
I-I CAN'T!

THE GENERAL GAVE THE KILL ORDER!
THE INFANTRY'S PROGRAMMING DOESN'T RECOGNIZE CONTRADICTORY ORDERS FROM LOWER-RANKING PEOPLE!

MILES! THE GENERAL!
HE'S THE ONLY ONE WHO CAN STOP THIS!
GOT IT!

KEEP THEM BUSY, LENORE!

YOU'VE LOST, GENERAL. SURRENDER.
NEVER!
BOOM
YOU WANT TO BE A HERO. I GET THAT. BELIEVE ME. BUT THIS ISN'T THE WAY.
LET ME HELP YOU. WE'LL BE HEROES TOGETHER.
B-BOOM
BOOM

THE WALLS... SO MUCH DAMAGE.
PLEASE, GENERAL.
A TRUE HERO WILL GLADLY SACRIFICE HIMSELF TO DESTROY HIS ENEMY.

MECHANIZED INFANTRY! COLLAPSE THE BUNKER!
BURY US ALL!

BOOMB

B-BOOM

BOOM

RMMMBLLL
THE WALLS ARE GIVING OUT!
GENERAL...

KILLING.
GETTING.
RUN!

WHOOMBLL

CRENNNCH

GO! GO!
GO!

WAIT FOR
MEEEE!

WE AREN'T GOING TO HAVE ANY TROUBLE OUT OF YOU, ARE WE, JERRY?
N-NO WAY.

GRAB ON TO SOMETHING!

CRMMBLLL

IT'S OVER. THE GENERAL... HIS ROBOT ARMY...
HE COULD'VE HAD EVERYTHING HE WANTED.
HE COULD'VE BEEN A *REAL* HERO.

CAN WE GO HOME NOW?
YOU BET, PARTNER.

CHAPTER 24

MILES KNOCKED ON THE DOOR OF APARTMENT 2H AS if he were a long-lost relative dropping by for a surprise visit. Which, all things considered, wasn't too far from the truth.

The group had ditched the elevator in some nearby woods and hoofed it the last mile to Cedar Lake Apartments, the cape draped over Miles's shoulder. Now, as Miles stood in front of the home he'd fled from a week ago, he felt more relieved than at any other time in his life. He heard fast footsteps approaching, and as the door flew open, Miles whispered a prayer of thanks. He'd made it home.

Mr. Taylor stood in the doorway, speechless.

"Hey, Dad." Miles smiled weakly. "I forgot my house key."

Mr. Taylor wrapped Miles in a bear hug so tight, he nearly squeezed the air out of him. "Dang it, son. Do you know what I've been through this week?"

Miles hugged him back. Indestructible superhero or not, there was nothing that could make him feel safer than being home and with his dad again.

"I've got the police and everyone I know looking for you." Mr. Taylor examined Miles from head to toe. "Are you okay? Are you hurt?"

"I'm all right." Miles said sheepishly.

"What on earth happened?" Mr. Taylor paused, his expression one of horror. "You *were* on Earth, right?"

"It's a long story, Dad. I'll tell it all to you. But right now I want you to know I won't ever disappear like that again. I made a lot of mistakes. I treated you pretty bad, too. Actually, worse than pretty bad." Miles choked back a sob. "But that's all going to change."

Mr. Taylor pulled Miles back into a hug. "Don't worry about that now. There'll be time for it later. I'm just glad you're home and safe."

After a long while, Mr. Taylor let Miles go. He looked at Henry, Lenore, and Dr. Petri as if noticing them for the first time. Three kids in orange jumpsuits, accompanied by a doctor in a lab coat. They must've looked like rejects from a science experiment. Which also wasn't too far from the truth. "We'll talk more about that later, though. Right now it looks like I'm going to be doing some entertaining."

Miles wiped the tears from his face. "Um, you already know Henry. This is Lenore. She has some kind of force field around her that stops things from hitting her. And this is Dr. Petri. She does research on aliens and other weird stuff."

Mr. Taylor offered his hand to Dr. Petri. "Good to meet you."

"Likewise." Dr. Petri smiled. "This is quite a young man you have here."

Mr. Taylor leaned toward Miles. "Did you tell them? I mean, do they know you're—"

Miles nodded. "Oh, they definitely know. Can they come in? We've been fighting killer robots at a secret army base all afternoon."

Mr. Taylor slapped a hand to his forehead. "That was *you*? The news is saying some kind of base got swallowed up by a sinkhole. I guess you're pretty tired, then. You all go on and find yourselves a seat."

Everyone filed into the living room. Mr. Taylor called Henry's parents immediately. Henry's mom screamed so loud for joy, Mr. Taylor had to hold the phone away from his ear. Mr. Taylor invited them to come right over.

While they waited, Henry insisted they recount the events while their memories were still fresh. He called it a "speed debriefing," which sounded like a fancy way of describing a locker-room prank.

As fast as they could, they each took turns telling Mr. Taylor what had happened to them, starting from the beginning. Mr. Taylor listened to it all without interrupting once. When they were finished with their story, he picked up a sofa cushion and tossed it at Lenore. The cushion skipped away before hitting her, seemingly changing course midair and knocking over a lamp on the end table.

"If that ain't the darnedest thing I ever saw," he breathed.

Dr. Petri adjusted her glasses. "I may have a theory about what happened to you, Lenore. About why you're able to do the things you do."

Lenore narrowed her eyes skeptically. "'Theory' sounds like you want to make me a prisoner in another lab somewhere."

Dr. Petri looked down. "Nothing like that. I promise. If you give me a chance, I can help you."

Lenore crossed her arms. "I want Miles and Henry in on it. I don't do anything without them."

Miles blinked. "You mean it? You want us to, like, hang out?"

"What?" Lenore huffed. "Is your little club boys only? Are we a team or not, doorknob?"

"Not just a team," Henry said, a smile spreading across his face. "A *super*-team."

Miles laughed. "I think that's a yes."

"I'd be pleased to have them join us." Dr. Petri was sincere. "Anytime."

Lenore nodded. "We'll talk."

Mr. Taylor cleared his throat. "So, what about Gary, the army guy? Should I be worried about a military raid on my homestead?"

"You mean Jerry?" Miles asked.

"Yeah, him. What happened to him?"

Henry piped up. "I told him Gilded had used mind powers on him, and if he ever thought about telling anyone about any of us, his brain would automatically liquefy and leak out his ears. He won't be an issue."

Mr. Taylor cupped his hands over his ears, looking at Miles nervously. "Do you have mind powers now?"

"No."

Mr. Taylor lowered his hands. "All right, then," he said, relieved. "Who's hungry?"

Food. Sounded like a plan.

Mr. Taylor went into the kitchen. Miles, Henry, and Lenore headed to Miles's bedroom to get cleaned up.

Miles and Henry went first in the bathroom, washing their faces and peeling off their jumpsuits. Then it was Lenore's turn. Miles handed her a pair of his jeans and a T-shirt.

"Sorry," he said. "I don't, you know, have any girl stuff."

Lenore wrinkled her nose. "Do I look like I'd wear a dress? Thanks for the clothes, doorknob."

Miles loaned Henry some clothes, too. They were baggy on his small frame, but he didn't seem to mind.

He left the bedroom and then came back with a garbage bag, stuffing his and Miles's jumpsuits inside. "My parents will be here any minute. We need a cover story."

The bathroom door opened, and Miles turned to talk to Lenore. "Glad you're done. You can help us come up with—"

Miles saw Lenore and caught his breath. She wore the jeans and T-shirt, and her hair was pulled back in a rubber band. Not high fashion by any means, but she wore it well. "You look . . . I mean, you're not . . ."

"You're *beautiful*," Henry cut in.

Lenore jammed her hands into her jeans pockets and looked away. She might've been blushing. "Shut up."

Miles nudged Henry. "The cover story, remember?"

Henry shook his head like he was chasing off a daydream. "Right. Let's get to work."

They came up with the story together. Miles and Henry had gone on a hike without telling anyone, then gotten lost in the storm. Somehow they ended up in the middle of nowhere, where they met Lenore, a runaway who'd endured one too many bad foster homes before finally making a go of it on her own. They all became fast friends, helping one another survive until they stumbled upon the campsite of the good Dr. Petri, who was conducting research on an invasive species of toad.

Rescued at last, Dr. Petri had promptly driven them all back to Miles's place.

Far-fetched? Sure. But Henry was counting on Mr. and Mrs. Matte being so overjoyed to have him back that they wouldn't ask too many questions. If they even listened to the story at all.

Henry went into the bathroom, stuffed Lenore's jumpsuit inside the garbage bag, then tied it shut. He tossed the bag into Miles's closet and dusted off his hands. "That takes care of everything."

Lenore stood in the center of the room as if she didn't know what to do or where to go. "Sure. Everything."

Miles felt guilty. He was home, and Henry's parents were on their way. But neither of them had stopped to think about Lenore.

Apartment 2H might not be a mansion and money was always tight, but Miles could sit down to a meal with family and friends whenever he wanted. Lenore had no family or friends. No home to go to. Miles swore he'd never take those everyday things for granted again.

"Don't worry, Lenore," Henry said. "You can come home with me tonight. First thing in the morning, my mom will call Social Services and set it up so you can stay with us until they find you a family. A good family."

Lenore rolled her eyes, as though she'd heard it all too many times. "And if they don't find me a family?"

"We'll figure something out," Henry answered

reassuringly. "Just think. All the trouble Miles and I got into, if it hadn't happened, you'd still be in one of General Breckenridge's cells. You might not have ever gotten out." He reached out slowly and grabbed Lenore's hand. "What I'm trying to say is, even the worst things can lead to something good."

Miles hung his head. He shuffled his feet, unable to make eye contact with either Henry or Lenore. "I know it's not just my dad whose trust I have to earn back. It's like I'm starting at square one all over again. But I've learned my lesson. You both can count on me."

Henry looked Miles in the eye, leaving no doubt that whatever he said next was the God's honest truth. "You've already got my trust, Miles. We're a team again."

"Not just a team," Lenore said, smirking. "A *super*-team."

Henry beamed. "You said it."

"No, you said it."

"Must be why it sounds like such a good idea. Now, enough of the sappy stuff." Henry patted his stomach. "I'm going to see how much food I can fit in here."

The Taylors, the Mattes, Lenore, and Dr. Petri—apartment 2H had never been so full. Dawn must've heard all the commotion because soon she'd joined their number too.

When Dawn laid eyes on Miles, she hugged him

almost as hard as Mr. Taylor had. "We were so worried about you. I didn't think I'd be able to keep your dad from losing his mind." Her hair fell over Miles's face, tickling his nose. "Thank God, is all I can say. Thank God."

Miles hugged her back. "Thanks for looking after Dad."

Dawn stepped back. "There's a new recipe I concocted. A twist on home fries. How does breakfast for dinner sound?" Dawn reached into the pantry and pulled out an onion. It might even have been a Vidalia.

"No!" Miles, Henry, and Lenore shouted in unison.

Startled, Dawn nearly dropped the onion on the kitchen linoleum.

Miles took it and placed it back in the pantry—way in the back, where he hoped it'd never be seen or smelled again. "What we mean is, breakfast for dinner sounds perfect. Just leave out the onions."

Everyone found a seat wherever they could and ate their fill, Lenore most of all. She seemed timid at first, like she hadn't eaten with a large group of people in a very long time. But once she realized no one was trying to get too close to her, she settled in and enjoyed herself.

If anyone noticed the boarded-up window in the living room, they must have figured it wasn't their place to ask about it. Which suited Miles just fine.

After everyone finished eating, Dr. Petri was the first

to leave. She left her phone number with Lenore and said she hoped she'd call. Everyone thanked her over and over, and she accepted the gratitude as though she really had rescued three kids she found wandering in the woods. Their secrets were safe with her.

The Mattes said their good-byes and started heading out with Henry and Lenore in tow. Miles wondered if she'd ever been in a house as large as the one where she'd be sleeping for the night.

"Steer clear of Henry's room," he warned her. "Or you'll get lost in the piles of laundry."

Miles held out his hand. Lenore studied it for a moment, then shook it. Gently.

"Thanks," Lenore said. "I mean it." It was the first time Miles had seen her truly happy. She had a crooked little grin, like she was sure of herself and unsure of herself at the same time.

"Anytime."

With that, their adventure ended.

After everyone else had left, Dawn hugged Miles again and went back to her place, leaving a kitchen filled with pots, pans, and dishes for Miles and Mr. Taylor to clean up. Small price to pay for such a celebration.

Miles washed and rinsed, and Mr. Taylor dried. Every clean pan, every sparkling dish made Miles feel more and more at peace. It was as though it were his mistakes and failures, and not food bits, that were being scrubbed away.

When everything was back in the cupboards, Miles and Mr. Taylor admired their handiwork. It was good to be home.

"I better call the police and let them know they can call off the search." He reached for the phone, then snapped his fingers. "Almost forgot." He pulled a scrap of paper from behind a magnet on the front of the fridge. "You got a few calls while you were gone." He handed Miles the paper. On it was scribbled a phone number and Josie's name.

Miles looked at the paper, unsure what to do. Last time he'd spoken to Josie, he'd been a total idiot. She was probably fed up and angry with him. He more than probably deserved it.

"She sure was worried about you. Called every day to see if there'd been any word."

"Really?"

"Wouldn't fib about something like that. Want my advice?"

Miles raised an eyebrow. "I thought wooing girls wasn't your strong suit."

Mr. Taylor looked offended. "You believed that? Shoot. First your mother and now Dawn. That's two girls I've gotten to talk to me in my lifetime. That has to make me some kind of expert."

"Okay, then. What's your advice?"

"Don't wait until you see her at school. A nice girl like that, you call her right now. No matter how much is on your plate, always make room for the people who care about you."

"I will. Thanks, Dad."

Mr. Taylor nodded. "You need anything else from me, just holler." He headed for the sofa and a return to the quiet, TV-filled evenings Miles was accustomed to.

Routine. Always a good thing.

Miles looked at the phone. He thought about telling Josie the truth about where he'd been and why he'd been acting like a jerk. What could it hurt to let one more person in on his secret? But that wouldn't be right. If Josie knew he was Gilded, she might forgive him no matter what. The way he'd changed lately wasn't because of the cape. It was in spite of it. Miles had to earn back her trust fair and square, same as with everyone else. No matter how long it took, that's exactly what he was going to do.

vrrrrrr

A familiar sound coming from an unfamiliar place—inside the kitchen drawer. Miles pulled it open and saw his cell phone sitting inside, where his dad must have placed it the night he'd flown out the window.

Miles checked the screen. The text was from Henry.

Priority-five incident. Tree fell over and downed some power lines.

Downed power lines. That was dangerous, wasn't it? High voltage was nothing to mess around with. What if the power lines were near a pool filled with kids going for a night swim? The cape was waiting in his room. It'd take only a few minutes for him to check it out.

Kids going for a night swim? That was his imagination getting away from him. Miles wasn't going to make up excuses to wear the cape anymore. When the city really needed him, he'd be there. Always. But in between, he was going to be there for the people who cared about him. That was important, too.

The power company can handle it, Miles texted back. *Talk to you tomorrow.* Miles thought for a moment, then added one last thing. *But if anything major happens, let me know.*

Miles dialed Josie's number. She picked up halfway through the first ring.

"Hello? Miles, is that you?"

Yeah, Miles Taylor was a superhero. But he was also Hollis Taylor's son, Henry's Matte's best friend, and Josie Campobasso's not-quite-boyfriend-but-definitely-something.

He was the luckiest kid in the world.